## She was shocked by what she saw in his face

Beyond the anger was a mass of pain and unhappiness, and Maggie instinctively reacted to it, forgetting everything that had passed between them in the last few minutes. She crossed the patio and raised her hand to caress the hard tanned cheek.

Jason stepped back as if her fingers had burned him. "Don't touch me," he snarled.

Maggie's voice was soft. "I...we were...."

"Lovers?" he asked harshly. "Is that what we were?"

"I...thought so."

"Anything to find out my secrets. Wasn't that it, Maggie? Didn't you want to know every little detail so you could telephone the police? Did you tell them how I made love, too? Was that part of your job?"

# Books by Claire Harrison

These books may be available at your local bookseller.

Don't miss any of our special offers. Write to us at the following address for information on our newest releases.

Harlequin Reader Service
P.O. Box 52040, Phoenix, AZ   85072-2040
Canadian address: P.O. Box 2800, Postal Station A,
5170 Yonge St., Willowdale, Ont.   M2N 6J3

# CLAIRE HARRISON

## dragon's point

**Harlequin Books**

TORONTO • NEW YORK • LONDON
AMSTERDAM • PARIS • SYDNEY • HAMBURG
STOCKHOLM • ATHENS • TOKYO • MILAN

Harlequin Presents first edition February 1985
ISBN 0-373-10760-9

Original hardcover edition published in 1984
by Mills & Boon Limited

# CHAPTER ONE

MAGGIE JORDAN was walking across Rideau Street enjoying the warmth of the sun on her head and bare shoulders when the wolf whistle reached her ears. It was long, low and emphatic. Despite the number of other people who were walking nearby, she knew the whistle was for her. Although she was not arrogant about her looks, she was well aware of the attention they aroused. She was tall, spectacularly curvaceous and very attractive; she had rich chestnut hair that swung on her shoulders, wide-spaced blue eyes fringed by long, dark lashes and an oval face that had a pleasing symmetry. When she dressed as she had today in an ivory summer dress with narrow spaghetti straps and a straight skirt with a short slit up the side that afforded an observer the occasional glimpse of a long, shapely leg, she had known the risk she would run in attracting male attention.

Maggie glanced over to the roadside where a construction crew was putting down pilons for a building, saw that the foreman was grinning insolently at her and walked over to him. She knew his type; he was large, brawny and macho. He thought he was god's gift to women. By the time she was standing three feet in front of him, his co-workers were hooting and whistling.

'Hey, Ron, what are you going to say to the lady?'

'Now you got her, what you gonna do, Ron baby?'

Maggie ignored them and stared at 'Ron baby'. She took off her sunglasses and slowly and very deliberately ran her eyes down him, from the top of his yellow hard hat, over the bulging muscles under the orange vest, past thighs encased in tight denim, right to the tip of his dusty brown construction boots. By the time she had completed looking the voices had died away although the grins had remained. Ron had lost his smile and was shifting a bit as if he were uncomfortable. Maggie waited until he looked her in the eye and then whistled. She had learned to whistle as a child, not the usual warble, but a piercing, shrill sound that carried for yards. She let loose with a long whistle that was unmistakable in its derision, watched the red flush rise in Ron's neck and then turned and walked away, her back straight, her high heels clicking on the pavement. Behind her, the laughter was raucous. Ron whoever-he-was, she thought with grim pleasure, was going to think twice before he treated another woman as a mindless sex object.

She was smiling when she entered the restaurant, a small and inexpensive Italian cafe in Byward Market, an area in Ottawa that was known for its narrow streets, tiny restaurants and boutiques. Oliver Henderson stood up when he saw her and said with an answering smile, 'Maggie, you look wonderful.'

Maggie kissed him on the cheek and then sat down opposite him at a table that was covered by a red and white checked cloth and had a white carnation in an imitation cut-glass vase placed in its centre. 'What fun, Oliver. I'm not used to sneaking to lunch with one of the top brass in the RCMP.'

'I'm not sure I'd call this sneaking,' Oliver said dryly, peering at her over the rim of his glasses. 'My secretary made the reservation.'

'Damn,' Maggie responded cheerfully as she opened the huge linen napkin on to her knees. 'I was hoping for something clandestine, top-secret and classified. We don't get much scandal at H&W. The closest we come is when a box of paper clips disappear.'

'And how is the job?'

Maggie had worked as an editor on in-house publications at the Department of Health and Welfare for six years, having moved up the bureaucratic ladder from proofreader to copyeditor to editor. While at first she'd been interested in the studies that were published; the incidence of certain diseases, statistics on poverty, grants and proposals, lately she'd become restless; her mind wandered during meetings, she'd read pages of proofs only to find that she'd absorbed none of it, she dreaded going to the office in the mornings. The truth of the matter was that she was bored stiff. 'It's a job,' she said, shrugging her shoulders and then added, 'Oliver, you must tell me what the occasion is. We haven't gone out to lunch together in months.'

Oliver accepted a menu from the waitress. 'I'm celebrating summer,' he said. 'I think it's finally arrived.'

Maggie smiled at him as she opened her menu. Oliver was her father's closest friend and someone that she had known for so long that she had always considered him 'family'. He worked for the Royal Canadian Mounted Police in some capacity or other; he never talked about his work. He was a short, trim man with a kind, avuncular face, and thinning brown hair. He smoked a pipe and wore rimless wire spectacles that tended to slip down his nose. He had always treated Maggie as if she were a favoured niece, bringing her candies and presents when she had been small and taking her out to lunch or dinner when she had grown-up. He had listened to stories about unfair teachers and skinned knees and, more recently, bosses, raises and job aggravations. Oliver had never married, and Maggie had always thought that she and her father had been a replacement for the family he'd never had.

'I'll drink to that,' she said. 'What's good here?'

Oliver adjusted his glasses. 'Everything.'

Maggie put down the menu. 'I'll stick to the antipasto—it's less fattening.'

Oliver gave their orders to the waitress and then turned to her. 'So you're planning to leave Daniel on his own in August.'

Oliver had been at the Jordan house two nights earlier when Maggie had announced that an old college friend, Carley Harris, had invited her to stay at her uncle's house on Dragon's Point.

'I'm going to hire a housekeeper,' Maggie said. 'Daniel is absolutely hopeless when it comes to the house.'

'You know, Maggie, you could stay at my cottage. It's closer to Ottawa and you'd be able to come home on weekends. He's going to miss you.'

'Now, Oliver, we both know that Daniel will not even notice that I'm gone. He has a paper due at the conference in September, and he'll be spending every waking hour scribbling equations.' Maggie opened the large napkin in front of her and spread it over her knees. 'Thanks for the invitation anyway.'

Oliver cleared his throat. 'If you're going to take a long vacation, why not go to Europe then? You haven't had much chance to travel.'

'I'd thought about it,' Maggie admitted, 'but then Carley's letter came. I haven't seen her in years and it was . . . well, an odd sort of a letter.'

Oliver waited while the waitress brought them their meals. He seemed deeply interested in his lasagna and asked in an idle voice, 'What did the letter say?'

Maggie speared a cube of cheese in her salad. 'It didn't say anything in particular; it was *how* things were said. It worried me.' There had been something in Carley's letter inviting her to Dragon's Point during August that had made Maggie decide to go. It hadn't been the words, a breathless, hastily-penned message, but something far more subtle, an edge of hysteria, an anxiety that seemed to emerge from between the lines.

'The black flies are terrible in northern Ontario,' Oliver said. 'You'll get eaten alive.'

Maggie put down her fork and looked at him. 'If I didn't know better,' she said, 'I'd think you didn't want me to go to Dragon's Point.' Oliver rearranged his glasses on his nose, and Maggie leaned forward, suddenly suspicious. 'You don't, do you?'

Oliver looked uncomfortable. 'You spend all year taking care of your father and now you're going to take care of a friend. It doesn't sound like much of a vacation.'

Maggie ignored that one; it was clearly a diversionary tactic. 'Why shouldn't I go to Dragon's Point? Is it a police matter?'

Oliver sighed. 'Don't let your imagination. . . .'

'Will it be dangerous up there? Are there criminals hiding in the woods? Is Dragon's Point a hideout?'

Oliver lifted up both hands in defence. 'All right,' he said, 'there's a possibility of danger.'

Maggie's eyes glowed. 'Really,' she breathed.

'I don't want you going.'

'Oh, no,' she said. 'You're not going to fob me off like that. What's going on up there?'

'Maggie, don't go.'

Oliver was dead serious, but Maggie ignored him. She was utterly sick of her life, tired of her drab office and the daily routine of a nine-to-five job that had lost its fascination months ago. There wasn't a man in her life, not since Nicholas, and she wasn't the type of woman who sought solace for an unhappy love affair in another man's arms. Carley's invitation had come at an appropriate time; when she needed to get away, when a month's respite from work would give her the chance to re-evaluate her life. Maggie had reached that state of boredom in which anything new looked good.

'I'm going,' she said. 'What's a little bit of danger?'

Oliver leaned forward and grabbed that hand that she had waved so nonchalantly in the air. 'Maggie, do you know what I do?'

She shook her head.

'I'm head of Narcotics Investigations.'

It took a moment for his words to sink in. Oliver had never talked about his work, and this was the first time

that Maggie had ever come up against the fact that the
professional Oliver was someone very different from her
father's chess partner. Someone who, on a daily basis,
dealt with some very nasty business. 'You mean—
drugs? There are drugs at Dragon's Point?'

'We're not sure.'

'Well, in that case. . . .'

'Carley's uncle is under investigation.'

'Carley's uncle? Jason Hale?'

Oliver was grim as he let go of her hand. 'Yes.'

Maggie was able to dredge up a number of memories
about Carley's uncle. They had considered him quite a
playboy during their college years, and Carley had often
regaled her with stories about Jason; there was Uncle
Jason jetting off to Hong Kong, Uncle Jason dating a
well-known film actress; Uncle Jason dancing the night
away in famous New York nightclubs. Although
Maggie had never actually met Jason Hale, she'd
formed a very definite image of him; blond like Carley,
bronzed by countless hours spent under exotic southern
suns and built like a Norse god.

'But he's a millionaire. Why would he be involved in
drugs?'

'His company, Hale Enterprises, is expanding. He's
into computer components and software and he's
looking for cash. We don't think he's got the resources
he needs.'

'But if you're not sure. . . .'

'We've got a man working undercover at Hale's
factory in Toronto. He's seen a well-known drug
courier going in and out. We think the drugs are
coming in from the Singapore company that assembles
his computer boards.'

'But that's just circumstantial evidence, Oliver. That
isn't enough to convict a man.'

'Maggie,' Oliver said with a sigh, 'I know that. We
need more to go on.'

'I'll be an informer for you,' she said. 'The RCMP

uses a lot of civilian informers; I read about it the other day in the *Globe*.'

'Your father wouldn't like it.'

Maggie sat back, suddenly wary. 'You wouldn't tell him, would you?'

'I . . .' Oliver paused and Maggie knew what he was thinking about. Anyone who'd ever been involved with Daniel Jordan came to the quick realisation that he inhabited a different world than most people. Daniel was a mathematician, an abstract thinker, a scholar and a professor. When he wasn't teaching he was busily writing books, articles and monographs about higher mathematics. His den was a nest of papers, books, journals and magazines, the surfaces of every table and chair littered with his scribblings and equations. He rarely descended into the world of ordinary reality except for meals and his chess games with Oliver. Maggie was quite convinced that Daniel had no real idea how to cook anything beyond a hard-boiled egg, clean a house, iron a shirt or take a city bus. Sophisticated though he might be on what must be one of the world's most ethereal and erudite topics, he was a true innocent in many other ways. If Oliver warned him about Maggie, Daniel would be flustered and upset, his owl-like eyes would grow round with alarm beneath his glasses, his fringe of white hair would seem to stand on edge. But he wouldn't have the first idea of what to do about it or how to stop her. Maggie had been making the decisions for both of them for years.

Oliver heaved a sigh. 'You're right. I wouldn't tell him.'

Maggie was triumphant. 'I'll keep my eyes and ears open, and I'll report back anything suspicious. Oliver, it's the perfect set-up. Jason Hale would never suspect that I'm a narc,' at this Oliver groaned, 'he'll think I'm just an old friend of Carley's. Well, I am. What a terrific arrangement!'

'Maggie. . . .'

She couldn't hold back her enthusiasm, but she was sure to lower her voice so that the other diners in the restaurant wouldn't hear her. 'I love it. I really do. I'm hired.'

'I refuse to let you. . . .'

Maggie grew suddenly serious and the laughter disappeared from her eyes. 'Carley is definitely in trouble, Oliver. She was divorced last year, and I could tell from the letter that she hasn't got over it yet. She begged me to come to Dragon's Point, and I have to go, drugs or not, dangerous or not. You might as well make some use out of me since I'm going to be there anyway.'

There was no mistaking her sincerity or determination, and Oliver knew when he was beaten. 'You'll have to be briefed,' he said with a sigh.

'Of course.'

'And I want you to phone me every third day. If you can't do it from the house, find a pay phone and reverse the charges.'

'Right,' she said.

'And so help me God, if for one minute I think you're over your head, you'll be out of there so fast your head will spin.'

Meekly, 'Yes.' Pause. 'What will I be looking for?'

'Heroin trafficking,' Oliver said. 'And it could be dangerous, do you understand?'

'Yes, Oliver.'

'Very, very dangerous.'

Dragon's Point hardly looked like a drug nest; in fact, it had an innocent, idyllic air, sitting as it did on a point of land overlooking Dragon's Lake. It had been built with an eye for the dramatic, nestled into the landscape with the soaring forest at its back and water surrounding it on three sides. Sunlight dappled its roof and cedar walls as it played through the low-lying branches of pine, poplar and birch; while, on the lake side, the reflection of the sun glittering in the water lit up the vast expanse of window. When Maggie had arrived, the first thing she had heard was the sound of water lapping against rock and the chattering of squirrels as they raced through the trees, their claws scrabbling over the rough bark.

Although Carley had called Dragon's Point a cottage, it had all the luxuries of a house; spacious rooms, central heating, a fully equipped kitchen and a bathroom that held a whirlpool tub and a sauna. Its most unusual feature was its shape. The house was hexagonal with screened-in porches on all sides so that its occupants could step out in three directions for a view of the lake or step out in three others to face the lush green foliage of the forest. Inside, all the rooms circled around the central living room which had a sunken carpet-covered centre and was lit overhead by a huge domed skylight.

'Fantastic, isn't it?' Carley said.

'Mmmm.' Maggie made appreciative murmurs as her eyes swept over the vast expanse of the living room with its grand piano, plush ivory carpet, dark brown and beige couches, accent pillows in terracotta and turquoise. 'Imagine building a place like this up here, nowhere from nowhere.'

'Merrick is only ten miles away.'

'Merrick has one gas station and a corner store. If you pass through it doing fifty, you miss it. Come on, Carley, this place is a hundred miles from any really civilised outpost.'

Carley stepped down into the sunken carpeted centre of the living room and flopped down on one of the couches, kicking off her sandals and laying her blonde head against the backrest. 'We do have a telephone and television and in-door plumbing,' she pointed out.

Maggie followed her. 'All the amenities of life but no neighbours.'

'Jason likes his privacy.'

Maggie sat down next to Carley and wiggled her bare toes in the plush thickness of the carpet. Although the summers in northern Ontario were billed as cool, the day was hot and muggy. She'd spent five hours in her car and then showered when she'd arrived, changing from her blouse and slacks to a halter top and shorts, but she still felt sticky and lifted up the heavy weight of her chestnut hair, trying to find a breeze that would cool the back of her neck. 'The mysterious Uncle Jason. Remember how you used to wonder about him?

'Wonder what?' Carley yawned and closed her eyes.

Maggie looked at her in surprise. 'If he slept with his girlfriends. What his sex life was like.'

'Oh, that small incestuous crush,' Carley shrugged. 'I grew out of it.'

Maggie's image of Jason had undergone several alterations since her conversation with Oliver. The blonde, good looks had remained but he'd developed an evil cast, an aura of dark secrecy hanging over his golden head. But now as Carley yawned once again, even that image faded to be replaced by someone stodgy and middle-aged, still handsome perhaps, but jaded from too much high-living or dissipated from excess. A man who had built this luxurious and isolated house to get away from it all *or* to conceal the fact that he was a criminal, the kingpin in a drug syndicate.

'I'm looking forward to meeting him,' Maggie said, but she injected a doubtful note in her voice.

'Are you?' Carley asked and then yawned again as if the subject of her uncle was a penultimate boredom. 'God, I could sleep all day.'

Maggie glanced curiously at Carley. She was beginning to wonder what it was that she had sensed in the letter, because nothing Carley had said or done for the past hour matched the almost hysterical tone of her written words. At her arrival Carley had greeted her with an exuberance, throwing her arms around her, hugging her tightly, exclaiming over her, but the liveliness had quickly faded to this yawning lethargy.

'Late night?' Maggie asked.

'Oh, the kind where you're wide awake for hours and finally doze off when the sun comes up.'

'Sometimes I have insomnia like that. But it's usually when there's something on my mind.'

But the probing, delicate though it was, came right up against whatever defences Carley had built against such intimate questions. For a moment the old Carley emerged again and gave Maggie an impish grin. 'Actually I spent the night thinking about your initiation into the world of black flies, poison sumac and mosquitoes.'

Maggie raised a slender hand in defence. 'I brought the Calomine lotion and 6–12,' she said. 'I came prepared.'

Maggie and Carley had joined forces at college when they'd both been freshmen, newly arrived on a huge campus and scared to death by the vastness of it, the standards of the professors and the sophistication of the upperclassmen. In those days, Carley had looked younger than she was, her blonde hair curling around her face, her brown eyes wide and having that look of constant amazement. Maggie was different; she covered her vulnerabilities with a false bravado and a hard edge, her long dark hair swinging down her back when she walked, her blue gaze direct, level and challenging. Their personalities had matched well; Carley, the carefree daughter of rich and overly protective parents, was in need of a guardian and Maggie was a caretaker by instinct. She had always been the type who managed, coped and organised, traits that she could trace right back to the day that her mother had walked out of the house and run off with a bachelor who lived down the street. Ten-year-old Maggie had learned how to run a house then, her small feet stepping into her mother's shoes with a surprising competence.

It was hard to say what Maggie would have been like had her mother behaved like other mothers; without her, Maggie had grown a tough shell, her only defence against the stares, the pity and the whispered comments of neighbours and classmates. She'd been bitterly ashamed of her mother and intensely protective of her father. As a result of hurt pride and a desire to show the world an uncaring face, she'd developed a bull-headed stubborness and a prickly exterior that turned away even those who wanted to be friends with her. If grade school had been difficult for Maggie, high school proved to be tortuous. She couldn't seem to mix in the normal adolescent world; she didn't know the first thing about what it was like to be a teenager. It wasn't until she met Carley that Maggie made the first tentative efforts to break out of her shell.

Carley with her flyaway blonde curls and quicksilver laugh had brought a type of excitement to Maggie's life that she had sorely lacked. It was adolescent and youthful, full of giggles and drama, and highly feminine. Carley had a tendency towards practical jokes, a high sense of style and a fascination for the opposite sex. She made friends at the drop of a hat and fell in and out of love like a playful seal that jumps in the water and then climbs out, shaking the drops lightly off before enthusiastically leaping back once more. Maggie saved her from umpteen scrapes and kept her from flunking out of school, but she also absorbed some of Charley's attitude towards life. Her rough, abrasive edges smoothed a bit; she learned to laugh; she even went out on dates and discovered men. Yet, not even a close association with someone like Carley, could erase the effects of the past. There was still a toughness to Maggie and a reckless courage that masked the fears and insecurity that comes from having too much hurt and not enough love. Maggie's father cared about her in his absent-minded way, but no one could replace the mother who had left without a message, a goodbye or even a backwards glance.

After graduation, Carley had got a job in publishing in Toronto while Maggie, electing to stay in Ottawa with her father, had gone to work for the federal government. At first, she and Carley kept in touch by means of letter, telephone and frequent visits, but over the years they'd come to see less of one another. Maggie was promoted to editor; Carley was married after a whirlwind courtship to a well-known stockbroker and then divorced with the same breath-taking speed. Their paths diverged, touching only at holidays when they might phone one another or at Christmas when they exchanged cards. Which was why Carley's sudden letter arriving out of the blue and begging her to come to Dragon's Point had struck Maggie as distinctly odd. She had responded to it both with curiosity and a resurgence of the old protective feelings. She had been unable to turn down what she had perceived of as a masked plea for help.

Carley had changed a lot in severn years, Maggie now thought, as she watched her talk about what they would do for the next three weeks. Nobody could have expected her to keep the fey innocence of eighteen, but the changes had nothing to do with the fact that Carley was, like Maggie, nearing twenty-eight. She was still slender, petite and blonde with a delicate prettiness, but her impulsiveness seemed calculated, her smile forced, the glow of her dimmed as if a light had gone out in her soul. Maggie couldn't help remembering the girl she had first met, the girl whose exuberance for life had been effervescent, bubbling over, enchanting and delightful. There was something about Carley now that brought an aching lump of sadness to Maggie's throat.

'. . . and I hope you like fishing,' Carley was saying, 'because it's our major form of recreation besides checkers at night. Dragon's Point is one of those places where you're up with the birds and asleep when the sun sinks. I come here when life gets too frantic.' She yawned again.

'And is it?'

'What? Oh, life. Maggie, you know how it is. Everyone needs a break.' Carley was talking just a little too quickly, a bit too glibly. 'Anyway we'll only have the place to ourselves for a couple of nights. Jason and Theodore are coming on Thursday.'

Maggie frantically went through the items in Oliver's briefing. Theodore. Theodore Wolfe, Jason Hale's accountant. Had worked for Hale Enterprises for fifteen years. A friend of the family. His wife had died six months ago. Maggie decided it seemed best to act ignorant. 'Theodore?'

'Haven't I mentioned Theo? Jason's accountant—a sweet cherub of a man. You'll like him.' Carley tangled a strand of blonde curl around one finger and threw Maggie a sideways glance. 'And David may come.'

'David—another business partner?'

'The latest fling in my love life. He's in the music business.'

'Do you mean he . . .?'

'God, I've been hogging the conversation. What about you? Your Dad okay?'

'Nearing retirement.'

'And men?'

Maggie thought of Nicholas and then answered, 'None at the moment.'

Carley twined her hands behind her hair and tilted her head to stare up at the domed skylight. A shaft of sunlight lit it at an angle, the beam carrying dancing motes of dust and bathing Carley in a golden glow. It touched on the shadows under her eyes, the lines of strain at her mouth, on hair whose blondness was no longer completely natural. She seemed to Maggie to be a fallen angel, tarnished and weary.

'Remember the old days, Maggie?' she asked wistfully. 'Remember Gustafson's Shakespeare class when we. . . .'

'Guns, Oliver, pistols, shotguns, Berettas.'

'What the hell!' Oliver's voice boomed in her ear.

'Just kidding,' she said. 'Actually it's so quiet here you could hear a pin drop in the middle of the afternoon.' Maggie was using the phone in the den while Carley was taking a shower.

'Maggie, this isn't a joke.'

She was sorry that she had teased him, but the trouble was she'd known he'd rise to the bait. 'I won't do it again,' she said soothingly.

Oliver's voice was gruff. 'All right, get on with it.'

'Jason Hale and Theodore Wolfe are coming tomorrow.'

Oliver's voice in the phone was brisk and professional. 'And your friend? Has she said anything?'

'No. I swear, Oliver, that she doesn't know a thing about it.'

He merely gave a grunt.

'Her boyfriend is coming. David—she didn't say his last name. Just that he's in the music business.'

'Okay, we'll check on that.'

There was a short silence and then Maggie said, 'And that's it, Oliver. I feel sort of silly. There's really nothing to report. Are you sure you want me to call in every third day?'

'Absolutely, and I don't care if you can't find anything to say except that the sun is shining. 'Oh, and Maggie. . . .'

'Yes?'

'I went and saw your father last night. He's fine and the housekeeper you hired is very organised. The house looked great.'

Maggie couldn't help her sigh of relief. 'That's good.' She paused and then added, 'Jason wouldn't be carrying a gun, would he, Oliver?'

'He's dangerous, he could be armed.'

'Oh.'

'Getting cold feet?'

'Of course not. I was just wondering.'

'All right. Now, remember, call me if there's the slightest hint of anything suspicious.'

'Okay.'

'And Maggie—take care of yourself.'

There was little in the house that really hinted at the identity of the owner and its occupants. Dragon's Point, Maggie discovered when she had poked around a bit during the next few days, was used primarily for recreational purposes; skiing and snow sports in the winter, fishing, swimming and boating in the summer. Jason Hale's imprint on the house consisted of a pile of old magazines, sports equipment of various kinds and several bookshelves of dogeared classics. There was a den, but the desk in it was virtually empty except for bits of stationery, pens, grocery bills from Merrick's small store and several old calendars. Maggie had gone through these, but they had yielded nothing except a furious blushing on her part. Jason Hale, it seemed, had once been the proud owner of the 1980 Nude Pinup Display in which every month was illustrated by a curvaceous, pulchritudinous fold-out. Maggie was far too sophisticated to blush over photographs of nude women in enticing positions. It was the words jotted along the bottom of several pictures that made her blink and then turn red. Bold, lascivious jokes regarding exotic sexual positions. 'Really,' she muttered, shutting the desk drawer quickly. 'Really.'

The bedrooms were equally uninformative. Oliver may have made a big point of Maggie keeping her nose clean and out of other people's business, but she couldn't see any particular harm in poking through the bedrooms while Carley was making dinner the next evening. She looked through drawers, shelves and closets and peered beneath the mattresses, but there was nothing to be found except that typical cottage paraphernalia—used paperbacks, boxes of games with their covers broken, hangers with the odd jacket or old sweater dangling alone in the closet. There was nothing, not even a hint, of drugs or the type of drug equipment that she'd read about in the booklets Oliver had given her.

'Maggie! Dinner's on.'

Maggie hurriedly pulled up the bedspread and straightened it with nervous fingers. She was in one of the bedrooms and she took a quick glance backwards at it as she walked out. Nothing was out of place, and she slowly closed the door making sure that it made no sound as it shut. Fortunately, the room was diametrically opposite to the kitchen, but all Carley had to do was step into the living room and she'd see Maggie walking out the wrong door.

'Mmmm, smells good,' Maggie said as she slipped into the kitchen. 'What is it?'

Carley was busy at the stove, brandishing a wooden spoon and a whisk. 'Chicken and don't ask what else. I never know until I'm finished.'

Carley, as it had turned out, was an excellent cook and preferred to have the kitchen to herself. Twice a day she would order Maggie to keep herself amused and then call her in to taste some delicious concoction. Maggie could hardly complain; she ran her father's house and her father with great efficiency, but it was wonderful to shake off the burden for a few weeks, sit back and let someone else cope with the shopping and making of meals. She had tried to help Carley, only to be shooed out of the kitchen. At first she had felt guilty, but within two days that feeling had completely subsided. Now, she had that pleasurably lazy sensation that comes from being pampered.

Maggie regarded Carley with affection. 'Since when did you learn to cook? When you were in college you could barely boil water.'

'Oh, I picked it up here and there.'

It was a typical Carley statement; vague and elusive. Maggie had quickly learned in the past two days that Carley wouldn't discuss the immediate past. She seemed to have shed some of her lethargy and Maggie thought she looked healthier, but there was no prying beneath the surface. They had hiked together in the cool of the mornings, sunbathed and swam in the heat of the afternoons and tried unsuccessfully to catch bass at dusk when, according to all authorities, they should be biting. Throughout all these activities Carley had steered the conversation in the direction of reminiscences of their college days, recalling professors, wondering about classmates, discussing boyfriends whose names they could no longer remember. And try though Maggie might, she could not force Carley to talk about her marriage, her divorce, her lack of a job or her latest boyfriend.

Carley dipped her wooden spoon into a pot, lifted it out and sipped, her eyes closed in judgment. 'Not bad,' she said. 'Needs a little something though.'

Maggie jumped up. 'Salt?' she asked, reaching for the salt cellar.

'Thanks. Now sit down and tell me all about Nicholas.'

'Nicholas! How do you know about Nicholas?' Maggie sat back.

'One time when I called you, your father said that you were out with Nicholas.'

'Oh,' Maggie said. She'd got the distinct impression that Daniel had not recognised Nicholas from one date to the next.

'Well . . .?'

Maggie didn't like to talk about Nicholas, but perhaps if she divulged something of her private life, Carley would be more forthcoming about her own.

'An affair gone sour.'

'Really? He sounded very glamorous—assistant to a Cabinet Minister.'

'He was,' Maggie said drily, 'a little too glamorous for his own good.'

'Oh—one of those.'

'One of those.'

'And since then?'

'Nothing.'

Carley turned around. 'I don't believe it.' She appraised Maggie in much the way she had tested her culinary concoction, with her head tilted to one side, her eyes narrowed in speculation. Finally she said, 'You've become quite sexy, you know.'

Maggie flushed. 'Carley. . . .'

I'll never forget the first day I saw you, standing against the doorway to Professor Devereaux's lecture. You were wearing jeans and that awful tunic top. Your hair hadn't been cut in months and you were an awkward bundle of angles. Do you remember how thin and lanky you were?'

Maggie gave a wry smile, 'Vividly.' She could also remember her painful ignorance of all things feminine. Her father was the kind of man that rarely noticed what a woman was wearing, and he hadn't been much help as Maggie had grown to womanhood. Without friends or a mother's guiding hand, she hadn't had a clue what to do to her hair or what to wear. Her choice in clothes had been often appalling. Not that she'd realised it until Carley had taken her in hand.

'Really, Maggie, you've improved with age—sort of like a good wine.'

Maggie gave a small, embarrassed laugh. 'I guess I'll take that as a compliment.'

Carley peered back into the bubbling mixture in the pot, pushing back a blonde strand of hair. 'Not all of us do. Improve, that is. Take me, for instance. I'm convinced that I'm past my prime.'

'Come on, Carley, that's ridiculous. You're only twenty-seven.'

'And have lived my prerequisite nine lives already.'

'Just because you're divorced. . . .'

Carley swung around and Maggie was shocked to see
the sadness written across her delicate features, filling
the soft brown eyes and turning down the corners of her
mouth. 'You're the tough one, Maggie. You're the
survivor type but I'm not. You see . . .' she began and
Maggie unconsciously leaned forward, thinking, thank
God she's finally going to talk and tell me what's been
bothering. . . .

But a door slammed and there was a jumble of male
voices and then the sound of suitcases and bags hitting
the floor.

It was as if a blackboard had been wiped clean.
Carley's expression immediately cleared as she gave
Maggie a smile and said in a mock-dramatic tone, 'Hark.
I do believe that Jason and Theo have graced the
doorway.'

A baritone voice range out. 'Anybody home?'

Maggie was standing up from the table when two
men appeared in the entrance to the kitchen. The first
was immediately indentifiable as Theodore. He was
every bit as cherubic as Carley had described, a small
round man with pink cheeks, grey thinning hair that let
the pinkness of his bald head gleam through and a jaw
line that disappeared behind his jowls. His eyes were
brown and expressive behind rimless glasses and he
sported a small brush moustache that looked incongru-
ous on his moon-shaped face.

No, it was the man behind him that stunned Maggie.
Of all the images she'd had of Jason Hale, none of them
came close to the man that filled the doorway. He was
neither blond and tanned, nor stodgy and middle-aged.
A thrill of shock ran through her, right down to her
toes. He had hair, dark as sable, thick and wavy,
matched by eyebrows that ran straight across a wide
brow, a strong nose with flared nostrils above carved
lips, eyes of an astonishing greenish gold between long,
dark lashes. Shoulders, broader it seemed than the sills

of the doorway, set off the leonine head while his body, tall and muscular beneath the white knit shirt and beige slacks, filled the room with a restless, animal vitality.

Jason Hale looked dangerous. He looked like the kind of man who was quite capable of running a syndicate and smuggling drugs, of carrying a gun and shooting it if the occasion demanded. When he glanced at her, Maggie got the distinct impression that he wouldn't suffer fools gladly and he'd be lethal if he had any idea that he was being double-crossed. She swallowed and discovered that her mouth had gone dry. While she had not quite pooh-poohed Oliver's fears that Dragon's Point was dangerous, she'd made light of them, not really believing that there was really another world beside her own, one with drugs and criminals and murders. Nor had she realised that the personification of evil could be quite so beautiful or have such a powerful and innate sexuality. It had never occurred to her that Jason Hale might be the kind of man who is dangerous to women.

# CHAPTER TWO

'AND this is Maggie,' Carley was saying.

The glittering green gaze covered Maggie from head to toe, taking in the striped blue and white bandeau that barely held in her generous breasts and the denim cut-offs that revealed her long and shapely legs. Maggie suddenly remembered those highly suggestive comments at the bottom of the calendar, and every nerve ending seemed to go into high gear under that intense scrutiny.

She held out her hand. 'It's nice to meet you.'

Fingers, long and warm, touched hers. 'I've heard a lot about you.'

Maggie had recovered her poise. 'Really? Don't tell me that Carley has bored you with all those bad jokes we pulled in college.'

'Let's see,' Jason said with a smile that revealed strong, white teeth. 'Didn't you french the proctor's bed, switch dates, sneak out after curfew, and . . .?

'No more,' Maggie said with a groan as she put her hands over her ears. 'Besides they were all Carley's ideas.'

But her last words were drowned out by the bounding, headlong entrance of a huge dog, a white Samoyed with a tightly curled tail, dark brown eyes and a mouth that seemed to be in a perpetual grin. 'Hercules, get down!' The dog had jumped up, put his enormous paws on Jason's impeccably creased slacks and was barking rapturously. 'Herc, old boy, this is no way to act in front of company. Meet Maggie.'

Hercules didn't even glance in Maggie's direction. He stared up at Jason in canine ecstasy, barked again and then grinned. He was clearly a dog with a single-track brain.

'He's hungry,' Carley said. 'I'll feed him while Maggie gets you some wine. The white is in the fridge. I chilled it.'

The minute Hercules heard the sound of Carley shaking a box of doggie biscuits he was at her side in a moment, staring up at her with equal adoration. Jason shook his head in mock-reproof at Hercules' betrayal and sat down at the butcher block table with Theodore while Maggie got the decanter of wine out of the refrigerator.

Theodore began to complain about Jason's driving. 'A maniac,' he said, 'whizzing around the corners, squealing his tyres, slamming the brakes.'

'Theo,' Jason said, stretching his legs, and Maggie couldn't help noticing the play of muscles beneath the now creased edge of his slacks, 'you're too nervous. I know these roads like I know the back of my hand.'

Theodore threw up his plump hands in mock-horror. 'Never again. So help me God.'

'Hercules loved it. Didn't you see how he stuck his head out the window and let the wind play through his ears?'

'That hound is too dumb to know what's good for him.'

Jason was amused. 'And how will you get out of here when it's time to go?'

'Carley will drive me.'

She threw him a wicked glance and shook her head. 'Everyone should have the experience of sharing a car with Uncle Jason. It fortifies the soul.'

Theodore's face expressed comic dismay at the way she had abandoned him. 'And to think I used to dandle you on my knee and bring you candy.'

'Not when I was twelve you didn't. We would have had you arrested.'

'Heartless,' Theodore murmured. 'It runs in the family.'

Maggie was finding it difficult to connect the things

she had learned from Oliver about drug running to this easy camaraderie and light-hearted banter. Heroin traffic was an ugly business, she had discovered, from the suppliers right on down to the street addicts, a chain of individuals marked by greed, avarice, corruption and venality. Yet, there were strong ties between Carley, Jason and Theodore; ties that came from long acquaintance and loyalty, from familial connection and affection. Perhaps it took a schizophrenic sort of personality to be involved in drugs, Maggie thought as she watched Jason's amusement; to be two-faced and with the facility to change with the wind.

The light ambience wound its way right through dinner, a fragrant Chicken Carciatore and artichoke salad which Carley served with panache. Jason toasted the month of August; Theodore toasted the doomed bass in Dragon's Lake; Carley got a little bit high on wine and talked non-stop, her delicate skin flushed, about the latest mystery novel she was reading where four people, two men and two women, just like themselves, were all alone in an English mansion and . . .

'The butler did it,' Jason said.

'I don't know,' she said, 'I haven't finished it.'

'The butler always does it,' Maggie said. She was enjoying the wine, too, and all thoughts of drugs and danger had gone from her mind. It was pleasant to be sitting around a table with people who were smiling and chatting, where the conversation meandered according to whimsy or caprice. This was her idea of a holiday: to get away from serious issues. She was tired of hearing about the machinations of the bureaucracy at work and chess strategies at home. She had lost all interest in the health and welfare of the Canadian people and she had never been able to have the proper respect for differential equations. And there was no denying the fact that sitting opposite a man as attractive as Jason Hale was having its effect. For the moment, it didn't seem to matter that he was under investigation by Oliver's narcotics' squad. Maggie had that heightened sense of her own femininity that a woman gets when an extraordinarily handsome man keeps glancing her way and his foot, occasionally? on purpose? touches her own when he shifts in his seat.

'And it is always the same butler,' Theodore said. 'He goes from one English mansion to the next.'

This struck Carley as very funny, and she laughed, her head thrown back, her long blonde hair swinging from side to side. 'Theo, you have a great sense of humour.'

Theodore smiled a sad smile into his wine. 'Like Petruschka.'

The sad clown—yes, Maggie thought, that was Theodore with his pink cheeks and eyes that squeezed into half moons when he smiled. Beneath the dimples and plumpness were sad shadows, and she remembered that his wife had died recently. A part of him had joined in with the fun, the laughter, the silly toasts, but she could sense that there was another part of him that remained separate, alone, unhappy.

Her thoughts were interrupted by Jason as Carley brought in their dessert; home-made pecan pie with cloudlike puffs of whipped creamed. 'Maggie,' he said, 'you're not a talker.'

'I'm listening.'

'Tell me about your job.'

'I've decided to forget about it for the holiday,' she said gaily.

Jason leaned towards her, the emerald eyes flecked with gold, his mouth curved into a smile. It was not the first time during dinner that Maggie had felt his eyes resting on her, but it was the first time that she had received the impact of his full attention. He was slowly twirling the wine glass in his long fingers and the glass gave off a glitter that made Maggie feel slightly dizzy. 'It's that bad, is it?' he asked.

'I am a bureaucratic paper-pusher. I am a cog in the slow wheels of government,' she intoned.

'But you earn a living?'

'That's what my paycheque tells me, although if you could see what they take out of it, you might wonder.'

'Taxes,' Theodore said with a nod, but Jason wasn't to be diverted into a discussion of Revenue Canada.

'And you live alone?'

'With my father.'

One dark eyebrow arched upwards, 'I see.'

Carley interrupted, 'Maggie is one of the most independent women I know.'

Jason's glance turned to her. 'Is she?'

Carley grinned at Maggie and gave her a sign of victory. 'Yup.'

His voice was suddenly dry. 'Well, at least she's doing better than you are. I'd like to see you working at least.'

There was a tension in the room that had not been there before. Maggie felt it immediately and looked quickly from Jason to Carley whose face had turned away, whose hands were suddenly busy removing a slice of pie from its pan. Even Hercules seemed to feel it. He had settled down near the doorway and fallen asleep, but now his big, white head lifted, his ears pointed and alert. The convivial atmosphere that had presided over dinner had dissipated with dessert. Maggie had the unsettling sensation of someone who has been riding along a smooth river, only to discover that beneath the glittering surface were whirling spots of turbulence, abrupt changes of current, jutting stones and dangerous shoals. Maggie could see a stiffness in Carley's back that hadn't been there before, a sudden wary tilt of her head.

'When I'm ready to work, I will,' she said.

'It's been a year,' Jason answered.

Theodore was trying his best to be soothing. 'Jason, it's been a hard year for her.'

'Work would take her mind off her problems.'

'Work would put me under more stress. My analyst told me to rest, take it easy, find my own pace.'

'Your analyst doesn't know what's good for you.'

Carley's chin lifted. 'And I suppose you do,' she said defiantly.

'Yes,' Jason said curtly, 'I do.'

Dinner ended shortly after that although, for all intents and purposes, it had ended with Carley and Jason's argument. An uncomfortable silence had followed while everyone quickly finished their pie and then went their separate ways. Maggie insisted on cleaning up the dishes, Jason and Theodore went to unpack and Carley disappeared into her bedroom. The house was quiet when Maggie had put away the last pot and, slipping a sweater over her shoulders, she stepped out the back door and walked down the narrow, pine-needled path that led to the lake. Dusk had already settled and the sun was an orange semi-circle on the horizon, reflecting jagged golden spears in the dark water of the lake. Overhead the trees murmured with the breeze, a conversation laden with soft brushing sounds and the creaking of branches.

The way to the lake was rocky and she was forced to step carefully so she wouldn't hurt the bottoms of her feet. Beneath her soles, leaves crackled and twigs bent; her arms brushed against bushes whose branches were so thin that their length merged with the dusk and were indistinguishable from the air. It was a time of day that Maggie particularly liked in the country, when the diurnal sounds gave way to nightly ones. Crickets chirped in the long grasses, a loon cried its lonely cry over the water and, when she reached the lake, she saw a small, dark shape slip away behind a rock, a racoon on its nightly foraging expedition. Despite Oliver and Carley's threats about the insect life, August had so far proved to be an exemplary month. Except for the occasional whine in her ear that required a slap, Maggie hadn't been bothered with mosquitoes.

The wind lifted her hair as she sat down on a smooth stone, and Maggie pulled her sweater close around her. She was not only chilled by the oncoming night air but by the scene that had occurred at dinner, the sudden disintegration of what had been a happy evening. For the first time, she wondered why Carley had come to Dragon's Point. She must have known that Jason would also be there, and it was clear that an animosity existed between uncle and niece. Carley's parents had retired to Florida years ago, leaving Carley to live on her own in Toronto. Maggie guessed, from Jason's words, that he had taken it upon himself to act in the role of guardian to Carley. She knew how easy and tempting it would be for him to have done so—Carley's personality was the kind that seemed to beg for someone to step in and take charge. She so often gave the impression of helpless femininity, of disorganisation, of lack of purpose. The only time in the past two days that Maggie had seen Carley in command was in the kitchen.

Carley . . . Maggie's thoughts shifted to memories of Carley at eighteen; exciting, laughing, the future lying ahead of her, its path strewn with delightful gifts. Carley had had money, connections and looks. The gods had seemingly blessed her with every advantage a woman could have, but the promise of that glittering future had disappeared as if Carley had stumbled into a dark place and lost her way. Maggie wasn't sure where Carley had gone wrong. She didn't know whether Carley had given up her glamorous job with the television network or whether she'd been fired. Her marriage had ended almost as soon as it had begun despite the fact that Carley and her husband had had a mansion for a home, a wide circle of Toronto's élite for friends and enough money to take frequent vacations to Europe and anywhere else they pleased. Maggie remembered how much she had envied Carley when the postcards had started to arrive, quick messages jotted down on the reverse sides of pictures of the Swiss Alps, the French Riviera, sun-lit Majorca, the Taj Mahal.

But somewhere, somehow, Carley's life had fallen apart. Her job had disappeared, her marriage had collapsed as if it had been an inflated balloon. She had lost her laughter, her quick spirits and her zest for life. And in its place was ... what? Nothing that Maggie could see except for the unknown David. Maggie had, unfortunately, developed an antipathy towards David. She couldn't put a finger on why she was sure that David wasn't the right man for Carley, but she was. Perhaps it was Carley's silence about him. It gave Maggie the impression that Carley was ashamed of him.

'Oh, hell,' Maggie said to the still waters of the lake, 'I can't figure it out.'

'Can't figure what out?'

It took all the bravado that Maggie had not to jump up, scream or otherwise make a fool of herself. She turned her head slowly and saw that Jason was standing by a tree to her right, his figure almost merging with it in the darkness.

'How long have you been there?' she asked.

'Not long.' He stepped away from the tree and walked towards her. Maggie noticed that he had the ability to walk without making a sound. When she had come down to the lake, her feet had brought the path alive with snapping, crackling noises. Jason moved like a large cat; silent, predatory, sinister.

He sat down next to her, his strong profile a pale cameo against the dying sun, his dark hair merging with the blackness of the sky. Their shoulders brushed slightly. 'What can't you figure out?' he repeated.

Her voice was light, easy. 'Whether or not the fish will bite tomorrow. Whether or not I will sunbathe in the afternoon or go into Merrick and sightsee. Whether or not I will decide to tackle a novel or simply stare into the trees and contemplate my navel.'

His voice was equally nonchalant. 'Mmmm—given a choice, I'd suggest you reading the novel while I contemplate your navel.'

'Oh-oh, sounds kinky to me.'

'Navel gazing does have its erotic moments, particularly when you let your eyes m——'

Maggie quickly put up her hand. 'I'm too young for this conversation,' she said. 'I'll go sightseeing in Merrick.'

'Ah yes—you'll have your choice of dusty shelves of canned pop, smelly boxes of bait or bins of quasi-fresh fruit. Unless you'd prefer the gas station to the corner store. Old wrenches, perforated tyres, slicks of oil. . . .'

Maggie couldn't help laughing. 'You've convinced me. I'll skip Merrick.'

'Now, on the other hand, if you'd like to catch crayfish with me . . .?'

'Crayfish?'

'Miniature crustaceans—a gourmet's delight for a hungry bass.'

'Is that why Carley and I couldn't catch any? Because we were using worms?'

Jason made a scolding sound. 'Imagine offering a discriminating bass some worms. Disgusting.'

Maggie smiled into the darkness. 'Where's your faithful hound?'

'Hercules? He's asleep in the living room, dreaming of country smells and the rabbits he's going to chase. Herc is strictly a hedonist; he lives for the day and it's pleasures. If there's one thing my dog and I agree on, it's Dragon's Point. It's our favourite place.'

'When did you build it?' she asked.

'Three years ago,' he said, 'when I'd decided that there had to be one place in the world where I could escape from my company, from Toronto, from other people and their demands.'

Maggie didn't know why—but his last words made her immediately think of a woman. She decided to play ignorant. 'Your company?'

'Hale Enterprises. I'm into computers.'

'And Theodore works for you?'

'Since I spend most of my time travelling, Theo takes care of the home fires. He handles personnel, payroll, accounts, that sort of thing.'

'You're lucky that you have someone you can trust.'

She couldn't see his face or know what expression had passed across it, but his voice held an odd hesitancy. 'Yes,' he finally said. 'I'm lucky.' There was a pause and he added in a lighter tone, 'Now, tell me about Maggie the bureaucrat who lives with her father.'

'I'm an editor at Health and Welfare.'

'And your father?'

'He teaches mathematics at the University of Ottawa.'

'And you live with him full-time?'

'Yes.'

'No mother?'

Maggie usually told people that her mother had died when she was small. It was a statement that elicited a small amount of sympathy and then the conversation would move on to other, more comfortable, topics. But there was something about the darkness, the soothing sound of the wind easing through the trees and the light of the moon now spreading across the lake with the sweep of a ghostly brush that made her mother's departure seem of infinitesimal significance. And the man beside her was so still that the words would fall in the deep well of his silence and disappear.

'She left my father when I was ten.'

'And he got custody?'

Maggie's voice was low. 'She didn't want me. She just . . . left. I haven't seen her since; we don't know where she is.'

'An odd sort of a mother.'

How thankful she was that he hadn't suddenly burdened her with an unwanted sympathy or gushed with the injustice of it. She'd been through those scenarios too many times. 'My father wasn't the easiest man to live with.'

'I didn't say that she was an odd sort of wife, just that her maternal instincts weren't very strong.'

Maggie thought of Sandra Jordan who had dreamed of being glamorous, of the style magazines littering the house and the unused cosmetics jumbled in the bathroom cabinet. One of Maggie's strongest memories of her mother was of an evening when she was about eight years old. She had been seated on her mother's bed and was watching Sandra try on a new sweater, a cashmere one in the colour of hot pink. Her mother had been a short woman, plump and curvaceous; she had had the sort of face that is beautiful when a woman is in her prime, but ages badly, the skin drying out and the wrinkles forming at the eyes, mouth and chin. She'd been posing before the mirror, twisting and turning, studying her reflection and smiling at it in a strange, intimate way. 'You should have been a movie star,' Sandra had said to the mirror, and Maggie had leaned forward to stare at the woman there, the woman who was her mother and, in some frightening way, not her mother at all. She had been too young to understand that narcissistic smile or the seductive way her mother slid the length of her long, dark hair over one shoulder.

'No,' Maggie said slowly. 'I don't think she ever wanted to be a mother.'

'So,' Jason said in a brisker voice, 'we've now established a third known fact about the elusive Maggie. She's a bureaucrat, she lives with her father and she's a semi-orphan.'

'Unfair,' Maggie said. 'It's your turn.'

'What do you want to know?'

'Mmmm—what you do in your leisure time?'

'Ski, play squash, read biographies, take Hercules for walks and make love.'

'What . . . kind of biographies?'

Jason laughed then and all Maggie could see of his face was the gleam of white teeth in a pale oval. The sun had completely gone down, and the moon was rising; a round and bone-white disc with faint shadows on it that could have been the features on a face. The Man in the Moon, Maggie had thought as a child, and she had envisioned him as a little roly-poly man, smiling down at the dark curve of the earth and a tiny girl's face pressed up against a window.

'That wasn't the question you really wanted to ask, was it?'

Maggie pulled her sweater closer to her. 'That was a very provocative statement,' she said, 'but I refuse to be curious about your sex life.'

'Why? I'm curious about yours.'

'It's off-limits,' Maggie retorted. 'None of your business.'

'All right, then I'll tell you about mine.'

'No!' Maggie said hurriedly. 'I'm not interested.'

There was a soft laugh again. 'You did ask me what I did in my leisure time.'

'Why do men persist in talking about sex?'

'And why do women avoid it?'

'Not fair answering a question with a question,' Maggie said. 'You're not playing by the rules.'

'Whose rules?'

'Mine, of course.'

Jason laughed again. 'I like you, Maggie Jordan. You're refreshing.'

She wanted to say that she liked him, too. She liked the way he was flirting with her, the way his mind could quickly shift gears along with hers and the way he laughed, as if he meant it, as if what she said truly touched his funny bone. But Maggie's other knowledge of Jason held her back. She remembered the things that Oliver had said and that very first impression that Jason had made on her: that he was a dangerous man. She hadn't forseen that he would also be charming, but she had to steel herself against the potency of that charm. She didn't want to like a man who was quite possibly a criminal, running drugs that were ruining millions of lives.

'Did I pass some kind of test?' she asked lightly.

He shifted on the rock and their shoulders bumped. Maggie could not help suddenly feeling his closeness as a threat and she shivered slightly. If Jason noticed that trembling, he did not say anything. Instead, he seemed to ponder her words. Finally, he said, 'Yes, I guess you have passed a test of sorts.'

'Oh?'

'You'll do for Carley,' he said.

She glanced sharply at him, frustrated by the fact that the moon's illumination shed so little light on his expression. 'What does that mean?'

'I'm sorry about that little fracas at dinner, but I've been worried about Carley for a long time. She's aimless, she's wandering, she can't settle down. She has her inheritance and more than enough money to burn. The result is that she doesn't do anything except sit around and get depressed.' His voice sharpened. 'I've tried to talk to her, but all she says is that she wants to be left alone.'

'She won't talk to me either.'

'She might given the time. Look, Maggie, she didn't want to come here, and then I remembered how often she used to mention you. I suggested that she invite you and, for the first time, she seemed enthusiastic about something. I don't know what's been going on in her life, but she desperately needs a confidante and it's clear she won't let it be me.'

'She does have a . . . boyfriend.'

Jason made a sound that suggested he was clenching his teeth together. 'I'd rather not talk about him.'

'Carley said he might come up here.'

There was silence and then a muffled curse. 'Worst thing that ever happened to her,' Jason muttered.

'Who is he?'

'David Moss. He's a goddamned two-bit swindler.'

That shook Maggie and not only because it was evident that Carley had got herself involved with a rotten element. Adages came quickly to mind. Do pots call kettles black? Do people in glass houses throw stones? If Jason Hale was involved in a drug ring, who was he to question the morality of others?

'What does he do?'

'Oh, he's in the entertainment business. He's a promoter, trying to set up rock concerts and other music acts. He was indicted a couple of years ago on a bribery charge. They didn't get him then, but they will some day.'

Maggie tried to imagine Carley being interested in a man with a criminal record. 'It's hard to believe that Carley would get mixed up with someone like that,' she said slowly.

'Carley's taken to running in a bad crowd. I don't like her friends; I don't like the wild parties she goes to; and I don't like David Moss. If she isn't in trouble already, she will be soon.' Jason reached out and his fingers touched Maggie's hand, the one that was gripping the edges of her sweater together. She hadn't expected him to touch her and the feel of his palm made a shiver go through her. 'Talk to her, Maggie, will you?'

'Of course, I will. I . . . just don't know if it will be any help.'

Jason's voice was grim. 'Every little bit counts. That's what I keep telling myself, that every tiny bit of help will add up to something.'

'Cloven hoofs, a forked tail and horns on his head.'

'Maggie,' Oliver said warningly.

'You said you wanted a description,' Maggie said innocently and then relented, 'Well, he's really quite . . . he seems very . . . well, frankly, Oliver, I don't see him involved in drugs.'

'The first thing a person learns in police work is never to judge a book by its cover. You'd be surprised at what I've seen, Maggie. Think of the nice, quiet neighbour that goes berserk and shoots his whole family or the good employee who's been embezzling the company for years. A man's outward appearance is no estimation of his character.'

Maggie had been standing on the porch that overlooked the lake that morning and had seen Jason and Hercules playing together; the man throwing a stick out into the water, the dog bounding in after it. Hercules' retrieval of the stick had been marked by much barking and water spraying and Jason, who'd been dressed in an old pair of jeans and no shirt, hadn't seemed to care in the least. In fact, he'd got drenched, the water in droplets on the bronzed muscles of his chest and back, his hair damp and curling. He and the dog had tussled over the stick, tugged it back and forth, wrestled with it until Hercules had leaped up on him in enthusiasm and subjected Jason to a complete face-licking. Maggie, in her mind's eye, could still see Jason after that canine embrace, his head thrown back, his delighted laughter reaching up to the blue dome of the sky.

'I . . . suppose you're right,' she said slowly.

'So don't get lulled into complacency,' Oliver said crisply. 'Keep your eyes open.'

'All right.'

'And we've done a check on Carley Hale's boyfriend. He's a pretty unsavoury fellow.'

'Jason told me that he'd been indicted for bribery.'

'He's got his finger in a number of dirty little schemes. The Toronto police have been watching him for a while. When do you expect him?'

'I don't know; Carley wasn't specific.'

'Does she talk about him much?'

'Not a word,' Maggie confessed.

'Draw her out,' Oliver said. 'Jason's the big fish, but I wouldn't mind catching a few small ones in the net at the same time.'

'Oliver,' Maggie said in alarm, 'I wouldn't do

anything that would get Carley in trouble with the police.'

'I don't expect you to,' Oliver said soothingly. 'And she's clean as far as we're concerned, but think about it from the overall perspective. How long is she going to stay clean hanging around with a petty criminal like David Moss?'

'Not . . . long, I suppose.'

'You're acting in her interests, Maggie, believe me.' Oliver paused and then said, 'Have you talked to Daniel recently?'

'Last night,' Maggie said. 'He seemed fine.' Which was an understatement since Daniel had been so involved in a set of equations that he'd barely had time to talk to her, his voice sounding abstracted, his concentration obviously elsewhere.

'He didn't mention the heating bill?'

'What heating bill?'

'He found the file with the heating bills from last year. I've never seen him so upset.' Oliver gave a little chuckle. 'It took me an hour to convince him that the oil company wasn't gouging him for every last cent.'

Maggie could just see her father in his bewilderment and concern. 'Daniel missed inflation,' she said dryly. 'He hasn't paid an oil bill in ten years.'

'I shouldn't have calmed him down,' Oliver said. 'He checkmated me in twenty moves. Twenty moves!'

'Try the property taxes next time, Oliver. *That* might upset his chess game.'

Talking to Oliver left Maggie with an unsettled feeling. He made the smooth and easy atmosphere at Dragon's Point seem like a false façade for any number of dark and criminal activities. Yet, it was hard to imagine Jason as involved in anything more serious than trying to decide how to spend his next leisure hour. As far as she could see, Jason's activities were as innocent as the day was long. He went for walks, played with his dog, listened to the stereo, chopped wood, went fishing, fixed the rigging on his sailboat and took photographs of birds and flowers. He was up early in the morning and went to bed early at night. He smiled, chatted, avoided any arguments with Carley and played checkers with Theodore. If he was mixed up in heroin trafficking, Maggie didn't know when he had time for business. Every moment of Jason's day was taken up with innocent amusements.

In her own naiveté, Maggie had quite forgotten that there are more hours to a day than those in which the sun shines. Like the raccoons who came out after dark, there were other nocturnal animals who find the cover of night necessary for their activities, a fact forcibly brought home to her two nights after her conversation with Oliver.

She'd had a bad dream, nothing that actually fell into the category of a nightmare, but a dream sufficiently disturbing to bring her swimming up from the depths of a deep sleep. The conversation with Oliver had had its effect; her mind had been filled with odd, uneasy and incoherent images; chessmen moving around on a checkered board trying to avoid faceless men with guns, her father's blue eyes alarmed behind their round glasses, Hercules growling, Jason's smile turning malevolent as he reached out to grab her wrist.

She came out of the dream with her body covered in a light sweat and the sheets tangled around her. She pressed the light button on her watch to check the time and discovered that it was a bit after two o'clock. The house was silent around her and outside she could hear nothing except the lapping of water against rock. Moonlight streamed in through the curtain over her window, illuminating the chair with her robe over it, the half-opened cupboard door, the bedspread that she'd tossed to the ground in her dream-filled agitation.

For a while Maggie debated the pros and cons of

getting up and making herself some warm milk laced
with brandy, a time-proven method of getting herself
back to sleep. She knew it would have the desired effect
but, on the other hand, she didn't want to wake anyone
up and she was loath to leave the warmth of her bed.
The nights were cool in Dragon's Point. So she lay in
bed and tried to will sleep to come but, when she'd
rolled over for the umpteenth time, plumped her pillow
without satisfaction and discovered that her eyes didn't
want to close, Maggie surrendered. Her watch now read
3:06, and the room was bright enough from the moon
so that she could get out of bed, pull on her bathrobe
and get to the door in the dark without tripping over a
piece of furniture or stubbing her toe. Slowly, she
opened her door and was just about to step into the
corridor when she heard a voice coming from the
direction of the den.

The house was perfectly dark and silent except for the
low murmuring of that voice. Whoever was in the den
had not bothered to close the door, but neither had he
or she bothered to turn on the light. The voice was so
low that Maggie couldn't determine whether it was
masculine or feminine; nor could she make out a single
word. The only thing that she could discern was that
the voice was involved in a phone conversation; it spoke
in fits and starts with long pauses in between. Maggie
could feel her heartbeat pick up in a breathless
excitement when she realised why someone would make
a phone call in the dead of the night. Whoever it was
had a secret so profound that it could only be expressed
under the cover of darkness and in a house made silent
by others sleeping. And what else could it be but about
drugs? If she knew the identity behind that muffled
voice, Maggie would expose Oliver's criminal.

Tension beat in her temples and she felt sweat
gathering between her breasts as she slipped noiselessly
out of her door and pressed herself against the corridor
wall. The hallway was dark and she could see nothing.

All her senses were concentrated on the tactile and aural. Her hands touched the cold surface of wall; her feet sank into the carpet, the low voice was like a beacon in the blackness. Slowly, she inched towards the den, her mind trying to calculate distances and thinking that, if she were caught, it would be easy to explain that she was en route to the kitchen which lay three doors away.

From one of the bedrooms someone coughed and it made her immediately straighten, her heart almost leaping out of her chest. The voice paused too but then went on, and Maggie took a deep breath, expelling it slowly, willing her pulse rate to slow down. She could hear the blood throbbing through her veins, could now feel the sweat trickle down her skin and knew that, if she took her hands off the walls, they would tremble with fear, with her anticipation and with her breathtaking audacity. Oliver's warnings came back to her in a flood tide of memories. *Don't get too nosey*, he had told her during a briefing, *don't put yourself in a dangerous situation. You'll learn enough by listening and talking. Don't start thinking of yourself as a detective or some romantic character out of a mystery novel. Drugs are dangerous and the people who deal in them are killers. Keep your nose clean.* She knew he would have been horrified if he could see her now, slinking towards the den in the black of the night with a possible killer only yards away but, on the other hand, Maggie wasn't the type that frightened easily and she was desperate to know the identity of that voice. She didn't ask herself why this was so important to her that she'd risk her life to find out. She just had to know.

Suddenly, everything happened at once. The receiver in the den clicked as it was being put back in place. Footsteps sounded on the carpet. And Maggie, inadvertently, took one step too far, having forgotten that, just before the den door, there was a small table against the wall with a lamp on it. Coming out of the silence, the noise was absolutely incredible. The lamp

banged against the wall with a loud crashing sound.
Maggie lunged for it in the dark, missed and collided
with the table which fell over with a resounding thud.
She couldn't stop her own scream of surprise as she lost
her balance and followed the table to the floor. As she
went down, her arms flailed in the air like furious
windmills, and she couldn't help thinking in an ironic
way how right Oliver had been. The minute she'd
tried to act like Nancy Drew, she'd fallen flat on her
face.

Lights clicked on, doors flew open, there was a
mumble of concerned voices and short staccato barks.
When she finally opened her eyes, Maggie looked up to
find worried faces looking down at her; Jason's,
Carley's, Theodore's. Hercules was trying to lick her
face.

'Maggie! Whatever happened . . .?'

'Why didn't you put on the hallway light? This
corridor is so. . . .'

'Are you all right? Come on, now, sit up slowly.'

The last was from Jason who had his hands beneath
her shoulders and was trying to help her up. He looked
as if he'd just woken, his black hair tousled, his torso
bare, the bronzed skin gleaming in the overhead light.
He was wearing only the bottom half of a pair of
pyjamas. In fact, they all looked as if her crash fall had
brought them out of a deep sleep. Theodore's spectacles
were sitting at an angle on his nose; Carley couldn't
help yawning. Not one of them looked as if they'd spent
a portion of the night making a clandestine and
possibly criminal phone call.

'I was just . . . going to the kitchen to get some milk,'
she said as she pulled herself upright. 'I didn't want to
wake anyone up.'

'The hallway is dangerous in the dark,' Theodore
said.

'It needs a night light,' Carley added.

Jason was still holding on to Maggie, his hands warm

through the thin fabric of her robe and nightgown. 'Are you okay?'

She gave him a wan smile. 'Fine,' she said and then, reaching out her arms, wiggled her fingers in demonstration. 'No broken bones. A few bruises maybe, but nothing serious.'

He let go of her then. 'You're sure?'

They stared at one another for a second, and Maggie felt a blush rise to her cheeks, not because she'd been caught in an embarrassing situation, but because it seemed that Jason could look into her mind and see the confusion his closeness had caused. If she moved her fingers the distance of only an inch, she could trace the line of black body hair that ran from the expanse of his chest down to the low-slung waistband of his pyjamas.

Maggie cleared her throat. 'Yes,' she said.

Theodore and Carley were straightening up the table and lamp, remarking how lucky they were that the bulb hadn't broken. Within minutes, the house was back to normal and everyone had gone back to bed. It wasn't until the first rays of light came through Maggie's window and touched upon her eyes, their surfaces feeling dry and tired after so many hours of being awake, that the thought of Hercules came to her. The dog was playful, energetic and noisy when people were up and about. Unless the Samoyed was an unusually heavy sleeper, nobody could have sneaked into the den without waking him and risking his barking enthusiasm. It struck her that only a commanding hand had stilled him so that the phone call could be made. And Hercules was a one-man dog: Jason Hale's dog.

# CHAPTER THREE

JASON HALE was enjoying his holiday. The weather was terrific, the sky was blue and the sun shone down in golden benevolence. He could feel its warmth on his bare back as he lay on the rock and watched Maggie turning over stones at the lake's edge. He eyed her lazily but with the sort of appreciation that a man feels when he is in the presence of a woman whose form stirs his blood and sends his thoughts in pleasing and lustful directions. She was wearing brief, blue shorts and a dark blue t-shirt with a v-neck. Her legs were long, shapely and tanned; the curve at the back of her shorts was tight and slim; her breasts strained against the fabric of her t-shirt. She wasn't wearing a bra, and he could see the outline of her nipples; small, enticing circles. Although her hair had been pulled up in the back in a clip, tendrils curled against the dampness of her skin at the neck and temple. She was sweating slightly in the heat of the afternoon sun and the flushed sheen on her skin reminded him of the after effects of lovemaking. He felt his body register this knowledge, and he was forced to shift on the stone to accommodate that familiar pressure.

Jason had known more women than he cared to think about. He had grown to maturity quickly. By the time he was sixteen, he'd been tall, muscular and appealing not only to the girls in his classes at school but also to women his mother's age. His first lover, in fact, had been one of her closest friends, a lonely divorcee who had ostensibly hired him to mow her lawn and then seduced him when he came to collect his pay. Their affair had lasted until his high school graduation and his departure for college. They had parted as good

47

friends, and Jason remembered her with a great
fondness and a silently spoken thanks. From her, he
had learned how to be patient, how to please a woman
and how to appreciate the subtleties of lovemaking,
lessons that had allowed him to enter more beds than
most men dreamed of.

His twenties had been a time of ravenous sexual
appetite, a time when Jason had gone through women
with an unsurpassed enthusiasm and an almost
complete lack of taste. The world had struck him then
as overflowing in its generous bounty of female flesh, a
department store stocked to the ceiling with women;
tall, short, blonde, brown-haired, slight and voluptuous;
each ready, willing, able and available if he approached
them with just the right amount of finesse and romance.
He had never tricked them, he had never promised
them any more than the pleasure of the moment, and
his heart had never been involved. As a result, his
liaisons had been as casual as they were frequent, a
kaleidoscope of legs and arms and breasts, of eager
faces and hungry mouths, of beds and tangled sheets,
not one distinguishable from the next.

Some time during his thirtieth year, Jason had
discovered an unexpected sense of discernment. He lost
interest in women as merely physical beings and began
to look closer, to become attracted to not only the way
a woman spoke but also in what she said. Once he
began to listen to the content of women's voices, he
discovered that he was not interested in most of them.
They chattered, they giggled, they made useless small
talk, they had inane opinions. A few women began to
stand out from the crowd and, with these, he'd had
several long-standing affairs. To his disappointment,
not one of them had developed in the direction he had
hoped. Over time, he'd grown bored with each of them;
Monique's political views had proved to be shallow,
Cynthia had had an unhappy childhood that obsessed
her, Diane ... well, he'd even come so close as to

consider marriage with Diane until he realised that her attraction lay in her intellectual brilliance only. Sleeping with her had never been as exciting or as interesting as her conversation. In fact, he had recently decided that, at the age of thirty-seven, he was jaded. He had tried it all; hot one-night stands, passionate flings, romantic commitment and a meeting of the minds. He believed now that he could look into a woman's eyes, see the gleam of attraction there and know, in advance, the entire course of the affair they might have, from the initial hedonistic moment right down to the last tedious day. And, in his most private moments, he had begun to question his own inadequacies, wondering whether his boredom really stemmed from the women he had met or was caused by some flaw within himself. This thought had caused him to declare a moratorium on the female sex. Although it would have astonished anyone who had known him, Jason had not slept with a woman in five months.

'Ouch! These things have pincers,' Maggie said as she held up a wiggling crayfish for Jason's inspection.

He grinned at her. 'Would *you* want to be bait?'

'Well,' she said, 'I suppose it would depend on what I was catching.'

'Now, there's a thought-provoking statement. It hints at the lascivious and even borders on the obscene.'

Maggie dropped the crayfish in a bucket while Jason admired the way the muscle in her calf moved as she bent her knee forward. 'I would be very discriminating,' she said.

'Meaning . . .?'

'Meaning that I would not put myself out as bait unless I liked what I was going to catch.'

Jason would have liked to sit up but his body was reacting, strongly, to the picture Maggie presented. She was facing him now, one hand shading her eyes against the angled rays of the sun, the raised arm lifting a breast so that he could see the fullness of it. Her legs were parted as she balanced herself on the rocks, and the stance was both militant and sexy, suggestive and defiant. Jaded and flawed though he might have been, Jason was not yet six feet under. Maggie's unconsciously arousing pose was having its effect.

He coughed slightly to detract himself and said in a dry tone, 'And I take it that you don't put yourself out as bait very often.'

'Rarely,' she said, 'there's not much worth catching.'

'Ouch,' he said with a wince. 'That sounds like a damning indictment of the male sex. May I hope that the present company is excluded.'

Maggie grinned at him. 'Certainly not,' she said and then began to move away. 'And catch your own crayfish. The ones I get are all mine.'

Jason watched her disappear behind a tree and turned over on to his back, smiling up at the sky. Maggie Jordan. Maggie Jordan. He tasted the syllables, rolled them around on his tongue as if they had a special and unusual flavour. His anticipation of Maggie Jordan had been a low one, an image evoked by Carley's description of years ago. He had envisioned a tall and lanky woman with little sophistication or grace. He'd been quite startled when he had arrived at Dragon's Point to discover that Carley's old college friend was beautiful and sexy with the kind of blue eyes that could make a man's heart turn over and curves that made his breath quicken. And the look she had given him had immediately hooked him; it had been cool and amused, questioning and enigmatic.

Although he wasn't arrogant about his looks, Jason knew the impact that he had on women. He was aware that some women's hearts melted when he smiled at them; others could be moved by a flirtatious glance, a touch on the hand, a sympathetic word. He had never been deliberately manipulative of a woman's affections; he had always been sincerely attracted to the woman of the moment and completely honest with her about his intentions, but he was also quite capable of turning on the full arsenal of his considerable charm when he wanted to make a conquest. Maggie had not quite responded in the usual fashion. Oh, she smiled and talked and, when he flirted with her, she flirted right back, that's as far as it went. He had the feeling that she had set an impervious barrier between them and it intrigued him. That, and the coolness of her and her quick mind and the long, clean lines of her body and blue eyes shaded by dark lashes and . . .

'Oh, hell,' Jason said up to the disinterested sun, to the indifferent dome of the sky and to the crow who watched him from the branch of a tree. He hadn't been worried by his unaccustomed celibacy; he'd even seen it as a necessary prerequisite to self-knowledge. He had used the time he would have spent on women to concentrate on his business, delve into books of philosophy and history, to try and make sense of the puzzling enigma that he had discovered in himself. He had discovered a need for a family, he wanted children, but he couldn't find the woman with whom he could share his life. He had wondered if he were too discerning, too jaded, too knowledgeable about women to find one that sparked his interest.

Maggie Jordan was the first woman in a long time whose conversation, whose body and whose smile had aroused him and a small flame of hope flared within his heart. He didn't dare blow it out of proportion; he was even cynical about the longevity of such an attraction, but its pull was too strong to be denied. He wanted her; he wanted to bring the smooth solidity of her flesh next to his, to seek out the soft desiring part of her, to bury himself in her sleekness and to penetrate the mystery of her. Jason didn't know how he was going to break down that cool reserve of hers or get past that secret amusement she seemed to feel in his presence, but he knew that he'd find a way. When it came to women, Jason Hale had never had a failure.

Maggie would have been utterly astonished had she known what was going on in Jason's mind. She knew that he was interested in her, but she had no idea of the impression she had made. She was far from indifferent to him, though the fact was that she was both fascinated and repelled by him. She often watched him in secret, enjoying the look and beauty of him. It was rare to find a man whose body and face added up to such an incredible perfection. Jason looked wonderful no matter what he was doing or where he had been. She had now seen him first thing in the morning when he was unshaven, the strong line of his jaw emphasised by a day's growth of dark beard; when he was filthy from cleaning an outboard motor, his body lean, muscular and almost naked in a pair of dirty denim shorts; and when he'd been swimming, his black hair sleeked back, his dark eyelashes throwing shadowy spikes across the tawny gold and green of his eyes. He had a grace and virility that few men possessed, and Maggie not only couldn't keep her eyes off him, she'd been forced to restrain an almost overwhelming urge to touch him. The bronzed skin seemed to ask for stroking, and the sable hair begged for fingers to twist their way through its strands. And his mouth . . . oh, Maggie couldn't bear contemplating his mouth. No one, not even Nicholas, had ever affected her in such a physical way.

But she was also frightened of him, and she wasn't used to being frightened of anyone. Maggie had learned at an early age how to take care of herself and, if that required confrontation in tough situations, then she was not one to shy away from facing an adversary or avoiding an argument. The fact was that she quite liked an incisive verbal battle and, when it came to flirting with the opposite sex, she was a past master at carrying on a sophisticated repartee. She was quite capable of talking circles around most men, and she knew how intimidating that could be. Nicholas had been the first man she had ever met who could answer her back, and

Jason was the second. She would have relished her encounters with Jason a lot more if she did not have reason to believe that, beneath the sexy, golden glance and appreciative masculine laugh, lived another, more sinister man.

Maggie knew what heroin did to addicts; Oliver had called taking heroin tantamount to a 'death wish'. It was the most addictive of all drugs and it sent its victims into an ugly spiral of urgent need, ill health and crime. Addicts would do anything to get their fix, from stealing to murder, and a vast underworld profited from their desperation with millions of dollars being raked off at every level of trade from the petty pusher on the street selling 'nickel' bags, five dollars worth of heroin cut with any innocuous white powder, to the kingpins who smuggled the drug into the country in its purest form. It was lucre and greed, ill-gotten and evil, and Maggie tried very hard, every time she looked at Jason Hale, not to see just the surface man, but to strip away that handsome mask and look to the man below, the one who was feeding heroin in the kilograms to a network of sleazy pushers and making millions off the backs of helpless addicts. Burglary, murder and even death from overdose could be laid at his door. It wasn't easy, but Maggie put Oliver's warning uppermost in her mind whenever she and Jason were thrown together.

Maggie did her best to stay out of his way, and she was most successful at this strategy when she spent time with Carley who also seemed determined to keep a distance between Jason and herself. She and Carley often took hikes around the lake, picnicking at whatever rock or inlet took their fancy, sunbathing and then swimming in the lake's cool water, diving off a stone into its dark green depths. Although Jason had bought acres of lake property, Dragon's Lake was large and there were cottages at the end where the shape of the lake looked like a dragon's head, and motorboats occasionally passed them, their occupants waving hello as Maggie and Carley waved back. Maggie's tan slowly improved, her skin turning a honey-gold, her eyes seemingly bluer for the contrast. Red highlights had appeared in her chestnut hair and a spray of freckles blossomed across the edge of her cheekbones.

'Dragon's Lake agrees with you,' Carley said one afternoon as they floated together, occasionally coming upright to tread water or paddle to another cool spot.

'Mmmm,' Maggie said. 'I don't think I'll ever want to go back to work.'

'And you've made a conquest.'

'A conquest?'

Carley gave Maggie an amused glance. 'If I didn't know you so well,' she said, 'I'd swear you were as innocent as the day is long.'

'Oh . . . you mean Jason.'

'So you did notice.'

'It would be hard not to; he's very . . . flirtatious.'

'Are you interested?'

Maggie didn't answer for a minute. She floated on her back, stared up at a wisp of cloud that was crossing the sun and felt her hair sweep back and forth in the slight swell of the water. She couldn't tell Carley the way she felt about Jason so she finally said, 'No.'

Carley was astonished. 'No? Jason doesn't turn you on? Most women go crazy for him.'

Maggie came upright and cleared her throat. 'That's the problem. I'm sure he bowls them over by the dozen.'

'And you don't want to be labelled as the next ten-pin?'

'Well, would you?'

Carley came out of her floating position and dunked her head back to get the hair out of her eyes. 'You're going to be a new phenomenon for Jason,' she said dryly. 'A challenge.'

Maggie slowly trod water, her arms weaving close to the surface of the lake. 'I don't intend to provide him with a victory,' she said. 'I don't play games like that.'

'I wonder how long it will take,' Carley said.

'How long it will take for what?'

Carley pulled herself out of the water on to a large overhanging rock and reached for a towel. 'For you to give in.'

'Carley! I don't intend to give in. There is no such thing as a totally irresistible male.'

'Jason comes close,' she said. 'Come on, Maggie, admit it—my uncle has to be one of the sexiest men you've ever met.'

'He's very . . . attractive.'

Carley laughed, the old laugh which showed that something had tickled her fancy. 'Maggie, you're so stubborn.'

'Looks aren't everything,' Maggie said primly.

Carley put the towel on her head and rubbed her hair vigorously. 'Jason is very charming—and he understands women; it's an unbeatable combination. He had quite a reputation at one time.'

'I'm not really. . . .'

'But he's cooled down a bit lately, sticking to one woman at a time instead of two or three. I didn't much like the last one; she was a brilliant lawyer, but she seemed cold to me. Who knows? Maybe she was passionate in bed.'

Maggie was about to reiterate the point that she really had no particular interest in Jason's love life; past, present or future, but her words stuck in her throat. The truth was that she was dying to know. 'Were they living together?'

Carley's hand tilted from side to side. 'On and off.'

'And . . .?'

'Jason doesn't confide in me. All I know is that it ended.' She finished rubbing her hair and, placing the towel down on the rock, lay on her stomach with her eyes closed. 'I was beginning to wonder if there'd be wedding bells.'

Maggie also pulled herself out of the water and sat on the rock next to Carley, letting the water stream off her and squeezing her hair out. 'Was she pretty?' she asked.

Carley opened one eye and gave Maggie a grin. 'So you *are* interested.'

Maggie stared at the lake. 'Only in the abstract,' she said.

'Rather than the flesh?'

'No matchmaking, Carley. I won't have it.'

Carley raised a protesting hand. 'Heaven forbid. Jason wouldn't listen to me anyway. As you've noticed, we're not getting along too well right now.'

Maggie seized the moment. 'He seems very concerned about you.'

Carley grimaced. 'You wouldn't know it, but beneath that gorgeous exterior is a man who is dying to be someone's father. When my parents moved south, Jason appointed himself my guardian angel. I'm a little old for a guardian angel, but he hasn't noticed that yet.'

'But you're not happy, Carley. Even I can see that.'

Carley turned over on her back with a sigh of impatience. 'What's happiness?' she asked. 'A husband, security, a job? I tried all that in spades and it didn't make me happy for a minute. Jason suffers from a work ethic; I don't. I have plenty of money and no need to earn a living. If I choose to find happiness going to parties and nightclubs, who is Jason to make a judgment on me? He's had his fun, let me have mine.'

Carley's voice had grown shrill, sharp and unhappy, and Maggie could see that she was going to have to tread lightly. 'Perhaps he . . .' but she didn't even get a chance to speak.

'The truth is,' Carley continued in an angry voice, 'that Jason doesn't like my friends. Just because they don't work from nine to five, he's decided that they're not fit to grace a Hale doorway. But I like them; when I'm with them I don't have to think.'

'Think about what?'

'About my life.' She sat up suddenly and faced Maggie. 'You're different; your life's gone on a nice even track. I've been married already, divorced already. I've had a wedding and an unfaithful husband. . . .'

The pain on Carley's face was suddenly so great that Maggie was scared for her. 'Carley,' she said soothingly, 'you don't have to. . . .'

'And an abortion . . . a horrible, awful . . . abortion.' The pretty, Dresden-like features crumpled as Carley began to cry. She had pulled her knees up and buried her head in her arms, the strands of wet blonde hair falling over her wrists.

Maggie was shocked. 'Carley . . . I didn't know.' She put her arm around Carley's shoulders, noticing for the first time how really thin the other woman was.

Carley's voice was muffled and broken. 'It isn't something you announce from the housetops.'

'When did it happen?'

Carley lifted her head, the soft brown eyes swimming with tears. 'When I'd been married about seven months, I found out I was pregnant. I was ecstatic about it; I thought Alex would be, too, but before I could tell him, I found out he'd been seeing another woman the whole time we'd been married. I hadn't even guessed, Maggie, it had never occurred to me that he had a mistress. I threw it in his face and he just laughed it off, saying that I'd always known he wasn't an angel. Well, I had known that, but I was such a naive little fool that I thought marriage would change him.'

'Why did he marry you then?'

Carley gave an unhappy shrug. 'He wanted the façade; he wanted children.' Her face twisted bitterly. 'So I punished him. I went and had an abortion and told him later. He was furious with me, he even . . . hit me, but I was glad I'd done it and told him so. I walked out on him after that and began proceedings for the divorce.'

'You're better off out of it,' Maggie said soothingly. 'He sounds like a monster.'

'But you see,' Carley said, 'I'd only had the abortion because I was so angry and so crazy with jealousy. I wanted that baby, too. I didn't know it until later when it was all over and it was too late. Maggie, it was half me, not only Alex.' She began to cry again. 'Don't you see what I've done! Sometimes I dream about the baby; sometimes I dream that I'm holding it and it's smiling up at me and we're happy and. . . .'

'Hush,' Maggie said and her arm tightened around Carley's shoulders. 'You're torturing yourself.'

As Carley wept, Maggie stared bleakly out at the lake. In the distance, a fish leaped out of the water and twisted in the air before falling back, a heron flew overhead, its long legs as straight as an arrow, and a bull frog croaked, its call echoed by another. Nature had intended a rhythm to human life, a rhythm of pairing and bonding and breeding. It had intended that Carley fall in love, marry and become a mother, but other forces had intervened: anger, violence, jealousy, revenge; disruptive and hateful forces that had broken the rhythm of nature, shattering Carley's own maternal feelings and causing her to destroy what would have been her own child. Whatever love Carley had held towards that unknown baby had been buried under an avalanche of other emotions, only to surface later. She was mourning, Maggie understood, grieving for the infant she would have held in her arms.

'If only I hadn't been so blind with anger,' Carley sobbed.

'You mustn't dwell on the past. There will be other babies.'

Carley shook her head. 'I'll never marry again.'

'You never know.'

'Maggie, I've been through it once. I know what it's like.'

'Alex wasn't a typical husband. There are other men.'

Carley gave her a bitter smile. 'I haven't met a nice one in years.'

'What about . . . David?'

'He's okay . . . he's useful.'

What an odd word, Maggie thought. 'Useful?'

But whatever defences Carley had let down to reveal the story of her marriage were now solidly back in place. She gave Maggie a quick glance and then turned away, her attention supposedly on the lake. 'As an escort,' she said. 'I need someone to squire me around.'

But Maggie had got the distinct impression that Carley was talking about something else, although she couldn't guess in what way a petty criminal could be 'useful' for Carley. Maggie knew that Carley didn't need money; she would swear on a dozen Bibles that Carley wasn't the sort to get involved in illegal activities. So she couldn't help wondering what was the attraction that bound Carley to the mysterious David. Perhaps she'd find out at another time, Maggie thought. Carley's reserves had come down far enough for her to reveal one secret and there was plenty of time for the revelation of others. There were still three weeks left to her stay in Dragon's Point.

But Carley's breakdown into tears had left Maggie with a sad and depressed feeling. To ward it off or, at least, to walk it into the ground, she decided to take a hike by herself before dinner and, since it was already getting cool, she changed into jeans and a plaid shirt. Carley was busy creating another masterpiece in the kitchen, Theodore was sitting on one of the porches reading a book and, from the tumultuous sounds coming out of the living room, it was obvious that Jason was playing the piano.

Maggie put her hands inside her pockets and set off to follow the edge of the lake in a westerly direction from the cottage. To her surprise, she discovered that she had a companion. Hercules came bounding along after her, his tongue hanging out, his curled tail wagging so fast it made a white blur.

'Don't you like Chopin?' she asked, looking down at him.

Hercules merely grinned at her, his ears perked high.

'You're a dog of small brain, my friend. All heart but small brain.'

'Woof,' he said.

'Well, now that we're in agreement, let's hit the road.'

Hercules had a particularly doggy way of hiking. He didn't travel in a straight line; he rushed from bush to dead log, from the lake edge to an interesting crevice. He buried his nose in piles of old leaves, on dirt mounds and on the underside of rocks. He studied the roots of big trees as if the secret of life could be found in their gnarled, knobby surfaces. An old pop bottle required a full minute of investigation; a stiff leather man's shoe without the laces brought on an ecstasy of tearing and chewing. And he would throw a backwards look at Maggie periodically to make sure that she too was enjoying the odoriforous wonders of Dragon's Lake.

Maggie was following Hercules' lead, but her thoughts were on Carley. She'd been appalled at Carley's unhappiness and horrified by her experiences. She could remember Carley's phone call when she'd got engaged, it had been full of excitement, anticipation and flying high spirits. Alex had sounded wonderful, the house they would live in was fabulous, their plans for a honeymoon had been spectacular. Maggie had missed the wedding by coming down with the most virulent 'flu of the decade, but Carley had sent her a photograph of Alex and herself standing before the church, confetti falling upon their heads like a shower from heaven. Carley had been radiant in white silk; Alex tall, handsome and distinguished in a dark tuxedo. He'd been twelve years older than Carley, but Maggie had thought the age difference was a good one. Carley needed the influence of maturity; the little girl in her had always remained a little bit too close to the surface.

But it was shocking to think that Alex had been far

from the man she'd envisioned. The successful stockbroker, the seemingly solid citizen, had turned out to be a philanderer and a wife beater. Had he married Carley because he thought she was so young and naive that she wouldn't notice the fact that he wouldn't give up his mistress? Or had it been merely a good business alliance for him? Carley had come into an inheritance from her grandmother when she was twenty-one and, although she had been working at the time, Maggie had always been aware of the fact that Carley was independently wealthy.

Poor little rich girl—that's how she would appear in a novel. An heiress born with a silver spoon in her mouth and all the advantages that wealth can bring. But none of it had made her happy. In the space of three years, she'd gone from radiant bride to bitter divorcee, a woman who had lost a husband, a baby and her expectations. Maggie could understand the despair that she saw in Carley's eyes; she could feel it deep in her own bones. And she knew how important it was that Carley talk about it, get it out of her system, air the grief that was tearing her insides apart to the point that she was wandering aimlessly through life, seeking any sort of fun she could find that obliterated, even for a second, that unspoken misery.

'Woof.'

Hercules was standing before her, his tail wagging like a metronome set at *vivante*. He had dropped a broken branch before her, his invitation for a game of 'fetch the stick'.

'I bet you've been playing this since you were a puppy,' Maggie said as she picked it up, 'and it's never even occurred to you that it's senseless, repetitious and not worthy of a higher canine intellect.' But Hercules didn't have a philosophic bent. He was dancing around her now, barking like crazy, eager for her to throw the stick. 'And if it lands in the water,' she added, 'I'll kill you if you get me wet.'

But the stick landed in the brush, was retrieved in an instant and returned with a great show and flourish. Maggie must have thrown the branch half-a-dozen times before she finally exceeded even her own expectations and hurled it into the lake. Hercules bounded into the water with enthusiasm and swam to the branch, picked it up in his mouth but, instead of heading back to Maggie who was preparing herself for the inevitable shower, he swam a hundred yards further to a small island and clambered on to the shore. He shook himself vigorously and then stood there expectantly.

'Come on, Herc, come on back,' Maggie called.

Hercules barked.

'Swim,' she yelled. 'Do the doggie paddle.'

Another bark.

'Come on, boy.' She picked up another stick from the ground and threw it behind her into the woods. 'Fetch!'

Hercules engaged in an absolute frenzy of barking, but he didn't budge and Maggie realised that he'd swum to the wrong shore by mistake and wasn't about to risk coming the whole distance back. She shook her head in disbelief. 'If you weren't so friendly and endearing,' she said, 'you know what they'd do to you?'

A wistful woof.

'They'd lock you up, that's what.' She glared at Hercules and then relented. 'All right, I'll get some help.' She could see Hercules tilt his head as if he were trying to understand. 'So don't go anywhere. Just hold on tight.' She started to edge away and Hercules shifted uneasily. 'I'll be right back,' she added hurriedly but Hercules only saw her disappearing into the trees and he started to howl in abandonment and misery, his muzzle turned up to the sky, the curled tail lying across his back in utter dejection.

'Your dog,' Maggie said, 'is stuck on an island out in the middle of Dragon's Lake.'

Jason had been playing a Chopin prelude when she returned, and for a second she had stood in the living room just listening to the lovely sound of the notes as they tumbled over one another, a musical cascade. She had also admired the pianist; he was so absorbed in the music that he had not noticed her arrival, and she was free to watch his frowning concentration, the agility of his fingers, the way the late afternoon sun gleamed in the rich darkness of his hair. But then he paused, noticed her silent contemplation and smiled so sweetly at her it had taken her breath away.

Now, he said, 'My dog is . . . what?'

'Listen.' Maggie waved towards the sliding patio door. Now that Jason had stopped playing, the faint sound of Hercules howling his head off could be heard over the chatter of squirrels and the chirping of birds. 'He was retrieving a stick and swam the wrong way.'

Jason grinned at her. 'Herc has a very bad sense of direction.'

'I noticed.'

They had to go after Hercules in one of the rowboats, and their arrival on the small island was greeted with canine ecstasy. Hercules wagged his tail so hard his entire back end quivered, and they could hardly restrain him from capsising the rowboat when he was forcibly hoisted inside.

'This dog is ridiculous,' Maggie said as she held the Samoyed at arm's length to keep him from licking her face. Hercules had been told to sit on the floor of the rowboat on the ride back, but his delight at being with Jason and Maggie was so great and his spirit of generosity so egalitarian that he had spent most of the time shuffling between them and trying to bestow small gifts of affection.

'"A very gentle beast, and of good conscience",' Jason quoted as he pulled on the oars.

'Shakespeare,' Maggie said, '*A Midsummer-Night's Dream*. I'll bet you need a lot of quotes to justify this animal. Down, Herc, down.'

'"The poor dog, in life the firmest friend, The first to welcome, foremost to defend".'

'Tennyson,' Maggie hazarded a guess.

Jason grinned at her, 'Wrong. Byron.'

Maggie wrinkled her nose. 'Byron would not have said that about Hercules—I'm sure he had better taste.'

Jason banked the oars and allowed the rowboat to glide into the shore below Dragon's Point. What you fail to understand is that Herc's stupidity is part of his charm.'

Maggie grabbed on to the oarlocks as Hercules, after giving her one more friendly lick, leaped out, causing the rowboat to rock at a dangerous angle and sending a spray of water over the stern. 'Charm,' she said slowly, wiping the drops off her face. 'There must be a new definition for that word—one I haven't come across yet.'

Jason climbed out of the boat, pulled it to shore and offered Maggie his hand to help her step out of the bow of the boat. 'Herc—I think she's insulting you,' he said, but the dog grinned at them with idiotic pleasure as Maggie stepped on to the shore. She tried to tug her hand out of Jason's grip but he held on to it, adding, 'Don't go. I want to talk to you about Carley.'

Maggie didn't want to stay with Jason, but she had promised to keep tabs on Carley for him. She glanced up at the windows of the house wondering if anyone there would be able to see the two of them talking, but the windows glinted back at her like huge, sightless eyes. 'All right,' she said with reluctance.

Jason dropped her hand and waved towards a large flat rock. 'Shall we sit over there?'

Maggie shrugged, 'Okay.'

At first Hercules couldn't decide who to grace with the pleasure of his company. Jason was sitting on the rock, his long legs stretched out before him, their muscular length encased in a pair of jeans. Maggie had lowered herself to the ground a few feet away and had pulled her knees up and wrapped her arms around her legs. The Samoyed looked from one to the other in perplexity and then finally opted for Jason, who buried his long fingers into Hercules' fur, stroking the dog's head and caressing his ears. Maggie looked deliberately away from Jason and towards the lake, watching the shadow of trees on the water, the delicate trail of a darting water spider, and the low dip and swoop of a swallow skimming the lake's surface. She refused to look in his direction although she could feel his eyes resting on her profile. She was far too aware of his physical presence—the tightness of the t-shirt over his chest, the curve of his bicep, the silky dark hairs on his wrist, the seductive motion of his fingers on Hercules' head.

'Have you had a chance to talk to her?' he asked.

'A bit—she talked about her abortion. It's made her so unhappy.'

'Yes, I know. I wanted her to get some counselling but she wouldn't go.'

'She's still grieving,' Maggie said. 'And she still feels guilty.'

'Damn,' Jason cursed under his breath.

'She talked about her marriage.'

'A disaster. I told her Alex wasn't the man for her but she wouldn't listen. She said she was madly in love.' The last words were said with a patent disgust and Maggie glanced at him.

'Maybe she was.'

'Carley was in love with an image of her own creating.'

'They say love is blind.'

'And do you agree?'

Maggie deftly avoided the issue. 'What a personal question,' she said lightly. 'You've gone out of bounds again.'

Jason's golden gaze passed over her. 'I'd forgotten,' he said, 'the rules of the game. Let's see—that leaves us with the state of Confederation, the impending economic doom or prosperity depending on your proclivities, international tensions and Nicholas.'

'Nicholas!'

'Ah,' Jason said, addressing the ripple of water that lapped up against the beach, 'the name rings a bell.'

Damn Carley anyway, Maggie thought. 'An old boyfriend,' Maggie admitted.

'One of many?'

'Out of bounds,' Maggie said sweetly.

'Tall, short, good-looking or a gnome?'

'None of the above.'

Jason's glance was amused. 'Hen's teeth,' he said, 'and they're pointed.'

Maggie shrugged. 'Let's turn the tables,' she said, 'and see if you like it.'

Jason leaned back on an elbow and surveyed her. 'All right,' he said. 'Shoot.'

The trouble was that Maggie was full of questions, and Jason was offering an open season on his life. There were hundreds of things she wanted to ask, most of which would arouse his suspicions, so she stuck to those that fit the moment. 'Parents?' she began.

'Retired, living in various warm locations around the globe. Presently on a cruise in the Caribbean.'

'Friends?'

'Enough to keep me happy.'

'Likes?'

'Mmmm—gourmet restaurants, Sunday mornings, a good newspaper, the colour blue, working with computers.'

'Dislikes.'

'Loud voices, cheaters, sweet wines, inefficiency, walnuts—I'm allergic to them.'

'Girlfriends?'

'Too many to count.'

That stopped Maggie and she gave him an unsmiling glance. 'You must be joking.'

'There was a time in my life when I didn't even bother to ask the woman's name.' Jason gave a small, embarrassed shrug. 'Thank God, I'm past that stage now.'

'You're glad it's over?'

'Contrary to the popular opinion of certain feminists, men need relationships that combine affection and respect and tenderness along with the more standard fare of companionship and sexuality.'

'It's nice to know your consciousness has been raised—at last.'

Jason grinned at the barb. 'Oh, I don't apologise for my twenty-year-old self. I was always courteous, kind and considerate. I didn't break any hearts, at least, none that I knew about.'

'And now? You didn't break the lawyer's heart?'

'The lawyer? . . . Oh, I see Carley has been talking about me. No, I didn't break her heart at all. She knew the end was in sight; we'd both tried our damndest to make the relationship work, but it had nowhere to go. Neither of us was under any illusions; there never was any real love between us. In fact, I've never loved any woman. I don't know why, but I haven't.'

Jason had been looking at Hercules during that speech, but now he glanced at Maggie. Her profile was to him; she was looking out over the water. Its purity touched him, the arch of her brow, the straight line of her nose, the delicate curve of her lips, pale against the darkening blue of the sky. He had meant to flirt lightly with her, to spark an answering flare of interest, but now he had the overwhelming urge to reach forward and touch the single strand of hair that had broken loose from her ponytail and curled in a dark wisp against the shell-like perfection of her ear. But when he did so, she flinched ever so slightly and quickly turned her head to look at him. Their eyes met and held, gold and green to a blue that matched the sky, and Jason's breath seemed to catch in his chest. She was so lovely.

'I'm being honest,' he said huskily. 'I'm telling you the truth.'

How could those blue eyes be so clear and hard when he had spilled out his guts to her? 'Are you?' she asked.

'Maggie.' He couldn't help the motion of his hand, it rose upwards from the rock on which it rested and gently caressed her cheek where freckles lay across the rosiness of her skin like a spray of miniature blossoms. She felt soft and wonderful to him; he could imagine touching the rest of her, sliding his hand over the silky warmth of her, feeling the bones beneath, knowing each angle and curve.

She hastily sat backwards, her eyes wide with alarm. 'Don't,' she said.

*Don't?* It wasn't a word that Jason heard very often and it almost slipped past him like a quick breath of wind. It was her look of surprise and alarm that made him speak, awkwardly because he wasn't accustomed to having to say the words. Most women understood the subtle messages, acknowledged them and willingly met him half-way. 'Maggie, I've been watching you and . . . I find you very attractive. I think you know how I feel about you.'

But she was scrambling to her feet, brushing the pebbles off her leg, nervously sweeping the loose tendrils of hair back. 'I have to go now,' she said quickly. 'See you—at dinner.' And with that she was gone while Jason sat in stunned silence, watching her mount the rocky steps to the house, her back straight and rigid, her hands clenched at her sides. He watched until she was out of sight and then stared for a long time into the blank space where she had been. Finally, he sighed and looked down at Hercules.

'I think that's known as a rejection, Hero, a real, live, honest rejection. You know, I don't think I've ever been rejected quite like that. It's humbling, that's what it is, deeply humbling.' He paused and Hercules, hearing the unhappiness and bewilderment in Jason's voice, licked his hand in sympathy. 'Maybe I'm losing my touch, maybe that's what it is. Five months of celibacy and I'm out of practise. The odd thing is, Herc, was that I thought she was interested, too. I mean I've caught her looking my way and I got those vibes, I really did. But tonight it was different. I could have sworn she was scared to death of me. Absolutely scared to death.'

# CHAPTER FOUR

THEODORE had joined Maggie for lunch on the patio that directly faced the lake, and they were sitting in a comfortable silence eating sandwiches from trays and watching the vista beyond the screened window. It had turned a bit cooler that morning and a light rain was now falling, its drops making small circles on the water's surface and drumming gently against the leaves of overhanging branches. The lake's wildlife had disappeared during this downfall, and there was no sound except that of the rain on the roof and trees and water. It was soothing, Maggie thought, to be sitting curled up on the wicker couch, sipping at a cup of tea and not having Jason's disturbing presence anywhere in the nearby vicinity.

He and Carley had gone for the afternoon, driving the fifty miles beyond Merrick to a town that had a decent grocery store. Carley had had a shopping list as long as her arm and had suggested that Maggie come with her so that they could investigate the local boutiques, but Maggie had refused. There was a new tension between Jason and herself; they didn't talk about what had happened on the beach two days earlier, but the knowledge of it was there, straining the atmosphere and making Maggie uneasy. The idea of sitting in a car with him and spending hours in his company was more than she could bear.

Her confusion over Jason had deepened and widened until Maggie's head felt as if it were spinning wildly through a mass of crazy facts and contradictions. Nothing made sense anymore. Oliver said Jason was running a drug ring, Oliver had said that Jason was dangerous, that he might be carrying a gun, that he could get violent. She had formed a vision of such a man during her briefings that had, admittedly, arisen from too many late-night thrillers. Maggie had seen Jason Hale as sinister, driven by evil impulse, his demeanour tainted by his secret profession. She had thought his criminality would show on his face like a scarlet letter and that his behaviour would be furtive and sly. She had never expected to find a man who was open, gentle, sensitive, caring and sexy. She had never, not in her wildest imaginings, thought that Jason Hale would be the kind of man who loved his dog, cared about his relatives, played Chopin on the piano, and could admit to a wistful uncertainty about his own ability to fall in love. And never, never, had Maggie ever conceived of the possibility that she might be physically attracted to him.

But she was; she had almost succumbed to him when he had touched her so lightly, the back of his fingers caressing her cheek, desire flickering in those magnificent golden-green eyes. She had felt his wanting of her as if it had been a palpable sensation like heat or cold. It had washed over her, demanding a response, and she had been shocked to feel an answering passion start within her, move like a coiled serpent deep within, spread through her veins with heavy pulsations. The feeling had frightened her badly; how could she possibly feel desire for a man who might be involved in drug dealing? and she had immediately backed away from it. But she still felt hot with embarrassment when she thought about the way she had walked off, leaving Jason staring after her, a look of shock on his face. It wasn't like her to be so adolescent, so awkward, or so lacking in grace. Maggie could hardly blame Jason for barely talking to her since and for glancing at her with a gaze that was cool and angry.

'Imagine,' Theodore was saying, 'almost two weeks of beautiful sunshine.'

Maggie picked up her glass of lemonade and sipped at it. 'Not even a cloud until today,' she agreed.

'So who cares if the fish aren't biting.'

'Right,' she said, 'the hell with them.'

Theodore smiled at her as he picked up his sandwich, and Maggie found herself wondering about him. He was such a neat little man, obsessive almost. His hair was parted precisely in the same line every day, he combed the few strands of hair left to him smoothly over his balding pate, he always smelled of a briskly scented shaving lotion. He epitomised, to Maggie, the accountant; he seemed fussy, controlled, highly organised. His trousers always had a straight crease, his shoes were highly polished, when he was finished with a newspaper, he folded it so carefully that the next reader could not have known that it had been read before.

He was clearly a man of strong habits and preferences. He teased Carley the way he must have teased her when she was a little girl, and his attitude towards Jason was a mixture of paternal and equal. From past conversations, Maggie had gathered that he had run his own accounting practice until Hale Enterprises had grown large enough to need a full-time comptroller. It was obvious that Theodore had been an advice-giver when Jason was young and newly in business, and he had stayed in that role even though Jason was now his employer.

Yet, despite the fact that Theodore was obviously one of the family, she was not sure why he had come to Dragon's Point. He wasn't much of a sportsman except for an occasional foray out on to the dock with a fishing line, and he seemed to spend a great deal of time reading in his room; at least, that's what Maggie assumed he must be doing. He never went swimming and only rarely sat in the sun. His path and Maggie's rarely crossed, and when they did, the exchange was full of polite enquiries and small conversations about the weather or the news. Maggie knew almost nothing about Theodore other than the bare facts of his life and that he truly appreciated Carley's cooking. And despite the smiles he often gave her, Maggie constantly caught a sad undercurrent in him, an unhappiness that verged on real despair.

'Jason tells me you're his right-hand man,' she began.

'My dear,' Theodore said, wagging a pudgy finger at her, 'you don't have to be polite with me. I deal with numbers and it doesn't make for exciting conversation.'

'I'm interested,' she protested. 'Really. I love numbers. My father's a mathematician, it runs in the family.'

Theodore picked up his cup of coffee. 'We should talk about the lake and the fish, the herons and the frogs.'

'But I'd love to hear what you do!' She didn't add that her underlying motivation was somewhat more complex. Oliver had told her about Jason's need for money to expand Hale Enterprises, and she wondered what Theodore knew about it and whether, in discussing it, he might offer her a revealing bit of information.

Theodore gave her a disbelieving look. 'I take care of Jason's books, look after personnel when he's travelling, pay the bills. I warn you it is very dry stuff.'

Maggie took a deep breath and stepped out into unknown and possibly treacherous territory. 'Then you'd know all about his plans for expansion.'

Theodore blinked at her over the rim of his coffee cup, his brown eyes alarmed behind the round frames of spectacles. 'Expansion?'

'Jason mentioned it the other day,' she said airily. 'It sounded exciting.'

The prissiness became exaggerated. Theodore pressed his lips together, his fingers met at the tips and formed a pompous, pontificating point. 'I don't like it,' he said slowly. 'I've advised against any form of expansion.'

But there was a sudden nervous quality to Theodore's small movements that gave Maggie the instinctual feeling that she'd hit pay dirt. 'Why?'

'I've told him it's too big a risk right now. The computer field is very volatile and he could fall flat on his face.'

'But surely Jason knows the risks?'

'I think he's been blinded a bit by his own success. I think he should stay put.'

'But if he has the capital . . .?'

Had Theodore gone a little pale or was the whitened look around his mouth a figment of Maggie's imagination? He cleared his throat. 'It's more complicated than that,' he said with a note of mystery. 'You'd have to spend a month looking into our books and six months of analysing the computer field to figure out the pros and cons of expansion right now. It would take me the rest of our holiday to explain it to you.'

Maggie realised that she had pushed Theodore as far as he would go. 'I thought it was simple,' she said.

'Heavens no. My dear, it's a very complex business.'

'Maybe, someday. . . .'

'Maybe,' Theodore murmured with obvious relief.

For a while, the conversation veered in the direction of abstract and safe topics. Theodore discussed the coming provincial election and the state of the government; Maggie idly touched on bureaucratic bungles. Then they discussed families, Theodore having asked Maggie about her father, and she talked about Daniel's work, his absent-minded behaviour, and the way it got him in amusing tangles. Theodore seemed relaxed then, chuckling at her anecdotes, so Maggie steered the talk in the direction of his private life and, in doing so, discovered a side of Theodore she had never seen before but only guessed at; the surprising and intense undercurrent of desperation that lay beneath his seemingly prissy and formal exterior.

'Do your children live in Toronto?' she asked.

'Scattered all over,' Theodore said, waving one hand in the air to demonstrate the fact that they were living in the four corners of the globe, 'a daughter in Calgary, a son in Texas, another in France.'

'You must miss them.'

'They all came back for Emma's funeral. Carley must have told you—my wife died six months ago.'

'Yes.'

'You remind me of her.'

'I do?'

The sadness in Theodore seemed to rise to the surface, causing his expressive brown eyes to turn doleful, the cherubic smile to disappear. 'She was shorter, smaller than you, but there's a resemblance in the colouring.' He looked down at the sandwich he had picked up as if he didn't know quite where it had come from and turned it over and over in his hands. 'She was really quite lovely, my Emma.'

Maggie felt awkward and uncomfortable in the face of his grief. 'Oh, Theo, I'm so sorry.'

He talked on as if Maggie hadn't spoken. 'It's hard, you know, to lose someone like that. She had cancer. We didn't guess for months, the doctors didn't know why she had the pain, they thought it was arthritis. Then when we found out it was already too late, too far spread, everywhere. Perhaps it was always too late. There's no real cure, you know, not for bone cancer.'

'What a dreadful. . . .'

But he wasn't seeing her or the gentle haze of rain or the beam of sunshine that had broken through the thick cover of cloud. Theodore had gone back to another, bleaker place where pain and sickness prevailed, to another, greyer time when the agony of his wife's dying had left permanent scars on his soul. The neat exterior of him collapsed as his face twisted with the memories. 'I kept her at home, I wanted her to be with her own things. That's the way Emma wanted it, too. I had a full-time nurse for her near the end. I tried to help her.'

Maggie didn't know how to handle these sudden and intimate confidences from a man that she barely knew, and she suspected that when Theodore remembered the way he had broken down before her, he was going to be excruciatingly embarrassed. But she realised now that all his careful organisation and precision were barricades against this wild grief inside him and that, like Carley, he had a desperate need to talk. It was as if that grief were overflowing, a single tear welling in a reluctant eye, spilling over in a sudden rush and tumult.

'Of course, you. . . .'

But Theodore had leaned forward now, his brown eyes on Maggie's face, his hands clenched together so tightly that the knuckles showed white. 'If someone you loved hurt so badly, wouldn't you want to help them?'

His intensity startled her. 'Yes . . . yes, of course, I would.'

For a second, Theodore watched her and, then, it was as if the spell had been broken. He took a deep, shaky breath, sat up, rubbed his pudgy hand uncertainly over his thin strands of hair and then gave her his sweet, cherubic smile that dimpled his round cheeks. He cleared his throat. 'I've been talking nonsense, haven't I?'

'No, not at all.'

'You're a good listener, Maggie. Has anyone told you that before?'

She shook her head and gave him a confused smile. 'No.'

Theodore glanced down at the remains of his lunch. 'Well, back to work.'

'Work?'

'Crossword puzzles,' he said. 'I brought six books of crossword puzzles with me and I plan to finish every single one.'

He neatly arranged the leftovers of his lunch on a tray, automatically straightened the creases in his trousers when he stood up and, saying goodbye, walked through the patio doors into the kitchen. Maggie watched him until she could no longer see his short form in the shadowy interior of the house and then shook her head in bewilderment. She was quite dazed by their conversation, by the sudden revelations and changes in character. She had thought she had Theodore classified, but now she saw that she was wrong. Perhaps the loss of his wife had unhinged him a bit, because he seemed off-balance, out of kilter and afraid. Beyond all the other emotions in him, Maggie had sensed that one. She didn't know what Theodore was frightened of, but his fear was evident, like the sheen of sweat on his skin when she'd spoken of Jason's plans for expansion and his trembling when he'd talked about helping his wife.

Maggie had always thought she was a good judge of character, having that innate ability to figure out a stranger on very short acquaintance, but this talent seemed to have gone astray at Dragon's Point. It had turned out to be a place where surfaces shifted and altered, where words could mislead and deceive, and where actions were never what they seemed to be. Maggie had the uncomfortable feeling that she was walking around in an imperceptible cloud that separated her from the others at Dragon's Point, making her eyesight less keen and her hearing less acute. Overheard conversations took on ominous overtones; events seemed to have more than one meaning. Even the sun, that golden eye, seemed to wink slyly at her in its blue canopy and, for the first time in her adult life, Maggie felt fear, not the sort of adrenalin-charged fear that comes of suddenly being confronted with a crisis, but an underlying and insidious feeling that forces were moving beneath the surface of normality, forces that she couldn't identify and didn't understand. And the worst of it was that she herself was changing; she could feel her own strong sense of identity breaking into chaotic pieces under the strain of confusion, the attraction she felt for Jason, the constant pull of Oliver's warnings. Maggie was discovering that, for the first time in her life, she was afraid and the person she was afraid of was . . . herself.

She might have calmed down and tried to put the past events into a more rational perspective, if it had not been for two incidents. The first occurred later that night after Carley and Jason had returned, dinner had been prepared and eaten, and everyone had gone to bed. Maggie had started to get undressed when she realised that she'd left the book she was reading on the living-room couch. She tip-toed out of her room, thankful now for the small light that was left lit in the corridor, retrieved her book and was heading back to her room when she heard voices coming from Theodore's bedroom. She glanced around her, saw that Carley's door was firmly shut and stepped closer toward Theodore's room and the narrow slit of his partially opened door. A ray of light angled towards the carpet of the corridor and touched on her bare toes.

'. . . to Sam,' Jason was saying in a voice that seemed to Maggie to hold a certain undercurrent of anger.

'I told you, he decided to retire.'

'Just like that?'

'It was a snap decision. Look, Jason, I didn't ask him why, he was close to sixty and it seemed logical to me.'

'He worked for me for ten years, Theo. Ten years and he didn't even bother to say goodbye.'

'You were in Singapore. We weren't sure when you were coming back.'

'And his phone's been disconnected. I stopped around at his apartment and he doesn't live there any more.'

Theodore's voice held a note of pleading. 'Sam's wife wasn't well; she wanted to move to a warmer climate. Yes, I remember now, he did mention something about retiring to Florida.'

'Where in Florida?'

'He didn't say.'

'He didn't leave a forwarding address either.'

'If I knew the answers, I'd tell you.'

There was a slapping sound as if Jason had hit his hand on a piece of furniture in utter frustration. 'I don't understand it. Sam was one of my most loyal employees; he was a good man.'

'Yes, he was.'

'Theo, are you sure that there wasn't something else behind it?'

'Like what?'

'I don't know, I can't figure it out.'

'He's only been gone for four months, maybe he's travelling, maybe he'll get in touch with you soon.'

'I wish I. . . .' Jason's voice trailed off.

'Wished what, Jason?'

'That I didn't think there was something fishy about the whole business.'

Was there a hint of nervousness in Theodore's laugh? 'What could be fishy about a retirement? Sam deserved it; he worked hard all his life. I wouldn't mind it myself. I'm getting close to sixty.'

Jason's voice carried a note of surprise. 'Theo, are you trying to tell me something?'

'No, ever since Emma, well I . . . work is all. . . .'

There was a silence and then, 'Theo, don't. . . .'

'I don't know if I can live without her . . . and she hurt so much . . . that's all I remember.'

Maggie heard the awful sound of a man crying and she could envision the scene in that room; Theodore hunched over on his bed, his face buried in his hands, Jason sitting beside him, perhaps putting his arm around Theodore's shoulders, trying to say the right things, trying to come up with the right combination of words that would ease a painfully hurting heart.

His voice had lowered to a consoling, soothing murmur. 'It was for the best, Theo. You know it was.'

'Yes . . . yes. . . .'

But Maggie didn't hear any more; she had pulled away from the door and was walking as quickly as she

could to her room. It was one thing to listen in on
conversations when she was playing the role of RCMP
informer, but it was quite another to be privy to a
man's intense and personal grief. Maggie slipped into
her bedroom and closed the door behind her, shutting
out the faint sounds coming from Theodore's room.
She sat down on her bed and stared, unseeing, at the
opened book in her hand. Part of the barricade she had
built up against Jason during the past couple of days
was breaking down again. She now knew why
Theodore had been invited to Dragon's Point and it
weighed heavily in Jason's favour. He had been kind,
generous and sensitive to the mourning of a close
friend. He must have known how hard it would be for
Theodore to take a vacation alone, his first without a
wife, and he had offered the other man his hospitality
and company. And for a man who had built this house
strictly for the purpose of getting away from the
pressures of business and acquaintances, it had not been
a small sacrifice.

Maggie slammed the book closed, sighed and wished
that Oliver had never told her about Jason. It would
have been so much easier if she were in ignorance about
his possible status. She would have truly loved her
holiday then, enjoying the house, the lake and the
attention of an interesting and very attractive man.
They might have gone canoeing together under the
dappled light of overhanging poplar branches or
walked together down the quiet paths of woods, their
hands running lazily over the vibrant green bushes as
they talked. They might be engaging in that playful sort
of flirtation that can make the day seem brighter, the
colours more tense and life infinitely worth living. That
flirtation might have even deepened into something
more. . . .

Maggie firmly put down her book, got into bed and
switched off the lamp on her bedside table. Idle
speculation was useless and non-productive. The truth

was that her expectations of a vacation at Dragon's Point had gone completely awry. She had only thought of the sun and lake; she had been prepared to have fun being a front man for Oliver, but none of it had turned out according to her plans. Carley, Theodore and Jason were driving her crazy, entangling their way into her emotions and leaving her restless and unhappy. Carley's problems had not proved easy to solve, she still obviously needed help; Theodore was cracking beneath his too neat surface; and Jason ... well, Jason was a frustrating and infuriating enigma. Maggie would have given anything to know what went through Jason's mind when he stared into space, when he walked down to the lake with Hercules at his heels and dipped his hand into the cool water, and when he looked at her with those green and gold eyes, their thoughts shadowed by those long, dark lashes. *Anything*.

The second incident took place the next day on an isolated and narrow section of beach along Dragon's Lake. Maggie had gone there alone when she stepped into the kitchen after lunch and discovered that Carley was in one of her extravagant, cooking moods. To Maggie, the kitchen seemed to be in chaos with bowls everywhere, half-a-dozen cookbooks piled up on the counters, pots steaming and bubbling, Carley's slight figure completely swathed in a huge white chef's apron.

'Out,' she had said when Maggie ventured in the doorway, 'I'm creating.'

'Creating what?'

'Ahhh,' said Carley in a mysterious tone. 'I never give away my secrets.'

'You're sure you won't want my help? I'm great at washing up.'

'Out.'

'But think of all the pots and pans and. . . .'

Carley had waved a wooden spoon at her in a menacing fashion. 'Out!'

So Maggie had put on her bathing suit, three tiny

triangles of black silk that were designed to expose more than they hid, and gone to sunbathe beside the lake. She lay on her stomach with her head resting on her arms and idly wondered if Carley's cooking binges didn't have something to do with her lost baby. Creation and genesis, she thought in a sleepy fashion as the warmth of the sun beat down on her back nurturing and feeding. . . .

A sandal scraped against stone, a cold canine nose nudged her arm, and Maggie looked up to find herself at eye level with Hercules. He licked her nose and she turned slightly to find Jason sitting down beside her, dressed in blue bathing briefs with a towel slung over his broad shoulders. The sun shone down and discovered dark blue glints in his black hair; a branch cast a shadow across his face, a line that reached down beyond one thick eyebrow, moved over the aquilinity of his nose and touched just briefly the deep indentation where the two equal curves of his top lip met. For a second, Maggie was insane enough to envy the shadow which could so easily and without detection caress that beautiful and unknowing face. Then she shook the madness off and tucked her head back in her arm.

'You found my hiding place,' she muttered.

'I let Hercules sniff your jacket and told him to find you.'

'I refuse to believe that your mangy hound had the brains to do that.'

'Believe it or not, inside that scruffy, white coat and behind those endearing brown eyes exists a fantastic mind.'

'Hmmmph.'

'I can't believe it—Maggie Jordan at a loss for words.' His gentle jeer was accompanied by a finger than ran down her spine, caught on the tie of her bikini, jumped over it and traced a line down to her hips. 'Dimples,' he said.

Maggie lifted her head. 'I'm sure you've seen dimples before,' she said in a cold voice.

Jason ignored her. 'Rarely there, darling.'

'I was sunbathing,' she said, 'and you've come and. . . .'

'You know, Maggie,' Jason said in a conversational tone of voice, 'I've been thinking about you and me.'

'There is no such entity as "you and me".'

'Sure there is, only you refuse to acknowledge its existence. I'm interested in you and you're interested in me.' He shook his head. 'No talking, it's my turn. Now, you can deny it until hell freezes over, but the attraction's there. It's coming though loud and clear to me, sort of like a bell ringing very clearly in the distance.'

'Hearing bells in your head,' she said sweetly, 'is a sign of insanity.'

'Sexual attraction is a sort of craziness,' he said softly. 'A wonderful craziness.' And once more, he ran his finger down her spine, only this time, when he reached her bikini strap, he deftly untied it.

'Jason . . .' Maggie began in a threatening tone.

'Now, take the bare back, for instance. He had leaned down on one elbow and turned on his side so that they were lying beside one another. Hercules had stretched out in the shade of a tree and dropped his head to his paws. Nothing moved around them except the soft motion of water lapping against the shore and the occasional buzz of an insect. 'There is nothing inherently sexy about a bare back; it's simply a collection of muscle and bone and ligament.' He gently touched her here and there with his forefinger to demonstrate. 'And skin is skin, isn't it?'

Maggie could feel the shivers skittering up and down her vertebrae every time he touched her, and the softness of his voice was having a mesmerising effect on her mind. Plus the fact that with her head turned sideways to him and with her face resting on her arms, Maggie had an exquisite view of masculine terrain; the column of his throat, the bulge of chest muscle, a dark nipple, black hair angling across a flat, muscular stomach, and that unexplored and enticing land beneath the blue silk that led to a pair of long, tanned legs.

'And since we're both consenting adults,' Jason went on, 'no one would stop us from indulging in a stimulation of . . . er, our backs. But every time I get close to you, I feel you pulling away. Even now, you're tense.' He touched the upper part of her leg, near the line of her bikini bottom, to demonstrate, and Maggie couldn't help flinching. 'See? You're afraid of me.'

She started to sit up, remembered almost too late that her bikini top was no longer attached and flopped down again. 'I've never been afraid of anyone in my life,' she said hotly. 'And would you please do up my top.'

Jason did nothing of the sort; this time, he caressed the curve of her waist with his entire hand, the warmth of his palm sliding over skin that glistened with sunbathing lotion. 'So I started to wonder,' he said, 'why Maggie Jordan would be afraid of an innocent character like myself. After all, I'm clean, I have no infectious diseases, I have perfectly good table manners. It's true I own a dumb animal who gets trapped on islands, but surely even someone as critical as Maggie Jordan wouldn't condemn me for my taste in dogs. And I don't want to sound arrogant, but most women seem to like me. I searched my soul and found it pure— lustful, it is true, but pure.'

Maggie was having trouble following the gist of Jason's conversation. The warmth of the sun beating down on her head, that gentle stroking of his hand and the deep murmur of his voice was having its effect. She felt dizzy; she felt an erotic heat start to build up in the centre of her, a spark of desire being fanned into flame; she felt as if she could have stayed there for hours, listening to him, and she closed her eyes as if to focus more intently on the sensations of sound and touch. She had quite forgotten all of Oliver's warnings about Jason

and her own apprehensions. She cared for nothing but
the moment; this slow, lazy and sensual moment in the
sun.

'And then I thought about Maggie and what sort of
woman she was, aside from being beautiful that is.
She's tough and sharp, clever and insightful, and I said
to myself, Jason, ole buddy, she's seen right into your
lustful soul and maybe she's scared of it. Maybe she
and Nicholas didn't hit it off in bed; maybe she doesn't
think that sex can be any different than that.' He
paused and then asked, 'You were lovers, weren't you?'
His hand moved up from her waist and stroked her
side, the tips of his fingers brushing lightly, accidently?
against her breast which was flattened by the ground
beneath her.

Maggie swallowed. 'Yes,' she said.

'And it wasn't any good?'

'It was . . .' This time, the fingers deliberately
followed the contours of her breast, along the swell of
its side, up over the top. For the life of her, Maggie
couldn't remember one single thing about Nicholas
other than his name. '. . . okay.'

Jason had moved closer to her; the hand that had
reached the top of her breast turned and exerted
pressure against her shoulder, forcing it up, so that she
now lay on her side, her head thrown slightly back, her
hair lying across one arm, her breasts exposed to that
golden-green gaze. 'And then I thought about your
mother,' he murmured softly. 'You told me that she ran
off with someone. Maybe that affected you—knowing
the power of sexual attraction and knowing what it had
done to your family. Maybe that frightened you.'

He hadn't even touched her bared breasts, but the
nipples, a dark and rosy pink, had already hardened to
aching points beneath his glance. Maggie was helpless
against the wave of desire that was passing through her
like wildfire, running through her veins, leaving its hot
imprint between her legs and turning her to liquid. 'I

don't know,' she whispered, and her lips remained slightly parted, their softness and pinkness begging to be kissed, her eyes darkened with passion, her body, still as it was, speaking to Jason of an erotic yearning, a longing for the sweetness of sex.

Jason had thought of little else but Maggie for the past two days; in fact, to his exasperation, he had realised that he was obsessed with her. He had tried to keep away from her, but had found that he was watching her, wondering about her, trying to figure her out. He couldn't guess what went on behind those tilted blue eyes or quick smile; he hadn't a clue what made her tick. His ability to read a woman's mind seemed to have deserted him, and he found himself lost in a confusing and foreign landscape. Without that inherent knowledge of the female thinking and the confidence that it gave him, Jason discovered that he wasn't sure what to do. He was a seeker without a map; a hunter without a guide. He didn't know what path would take him to Maggie's heart; she seemed inaccessible to him, walled-off, mysterious and elusive.

He had thought of half-a-dozen ways to approach her, discarding each as either too much of a come-on or ridiculous. He had, mentally, held long conversations with her, discussions that would break down that invisible wall she had built between them and soften that wary look in her eyes, but when he thought of actually mouthing the words that were in his head, he winced. They made him sound so adolescent, so much like the sixteen-year-old he had once been; gauche, shy and clumsy. Jason had tried everything he could think of, short of cold showers, that would take his mind off Maggie. He had worked on a Beethoven piece that had always eluded him; he had attempted to concentrate on a long history of the Boer War; he had tried to fall asleep at night by counting sheep. He was highly cynical of this 'infatuation', as he termed it, not understanding why Maggie was capable of reducing him, a sophisticated and mature man, to a miserable creature filled with romantic, teenage longings. After long contemplation, Jason had finally come to a rational conclusion; it was his celibacy that was to blame, being without a woman for so long had rattled his brains and sent his emotional index into orbit. The only remedy he could think of was satiation, and the means to that end was Maggie.

He pulled her into his arms, her breasts soft and warm against his chest. He was ready for her, but then she must know that, he thought, his mind dizzy with the closeness of her. She must be able to feel the hardness that lay between them, the burning heat of his arousal, and know how much he wanted her. She felt as good as he had thought she would, his hands making long caresses of her back, the sleek stretch of her side, the enticing curve of her stomach above the flimsy fabric of her bikini. He kissed that eager mouth, felt the shape of her lips against his, the ridge of her teeth, the wetness of her tongue. He left her mouth to explore the softness of her neck, the pulse beating in her throat, the delicate indentation where the inner wings of her shoulder blades met. He touched his tongue to each spot and tasted a slight saltiness.

Now, he was discovering that he loved the smell of her, that musky combination of sun and lotion and heat. And he loved the feel of her, the weight of her breast in his hand, the rough texture of a hardened nipple against his tongue. Her legs were tangling with his; their hips were meeting and he longed to slide within her. Yet even as he held her in his arms and could hear the rapid intake of her breath in his ear, Jason was aware that his possession of her would only be physical. He had a thousand questions he suddenly discovered that he wanted to ask her, a thousand things he wanted to say, but ... she wound her arms about him and raised her mouth once again to his, and his thought pattern heated and then broke altogether.

Everything was forgotten as their lips met, and he was pulled into a kiss that took him, a drowning man, deep into the swirling, gleaming sea of her.

The sun bathed them in golden rays, the lake rippled at their feet, and Hercules shifted restlessly and then stood up. He touched the back of Jason's neck with his nose and snuffled gently in his ear. To his delight, Jason slowly turned his head and stared at him. 'Disappear, Herc,' he growled.

The Samoyed looked bewildered and unhappy as Jason's tone registered in his doggy brain, as he attempted to seek forgiveness by licking Jason's cheek.

Jason rolled over. 'Jesus,' he breathed and then roared, 'Go away!'

But Hercules had a different idea. He sniffed Jason's neck. He placed his sandy paws on Jason's chest. He lowered his head to his paws and stared meaningfully at Jason's chin. He didn't know what he had done wrong, but he desperately wanted to be friends again. When Jason pointed towards the house and said, 'Go home!' Hercules glanced in the direction of that pointed finger, then back at that dearly beloved face and didn't budge an inch.

Maggie was making odd, choking noises. When Jason glanced over at her, he saw that she had pulled away from him and was quickly doing up her bikini top, her head bent, her dark hair falling beside her cheeks.

'Maggie,' he said, pushing Hercules off him.

'I have to go.'

'Maggie, please. Just as soon as I get rid of this. . . .'

She lifted her head then and he saw a mixture of emotions on it that struck him dumb. Hercules had made her laugh and there was still a shred of a smile left, but it was her eyes that riveted him. Tears glistened against their blue depths and dampened her lashes. Tears!

'Don't . . .' he began, reaching out for her, but

Maggie was already standing, her towel clutched to her chest. 'Please don't go,' he said desperately.

'I ... have to,' she said and, once again, she was gone, leaving Jason sitting at the edge of Dragon's Lake with his dog beside him. He watched her as she disappeared into the trees and then, sitting up straight, glared at Hercules who tentatively wagged his curled tail and gazed up at him with brown eyes soft with adoration. Finally Jason sighed and asked, 'What did I do to deserve that? Did *I* interrupt you when you were panting after that cocker spaniel? And what about that amorous adventure with the lady collie in Mississauga? Huh, Herc, what about that? I encouraged you, I took your leash off, and this is how you repay me. If you keep up this sort of ungrateful behaviour, I'm going to tie you up in the back yard and let you howl. Hear me?'

Hercules heard nothing but the sound of Jason's voice. He didn't know what he had done to deserve Jason's anger and he only dimly understood the note of despair that lay below Jason's words. What came loud and clear through the foggy mists of his canine brain was the undercurrent of laughter that told him he was forgiven. In utter relief, he licked Jason's face, a long, wet and very loving lick.

'Oliver?'

'Maggie! What's the matter?'

'I ....'

'Has anyone threatened you?'

'No, nothing like that.'

He took a deep breath. 'It's not your day to call.'

'I know but ... Oliver, are you absolutely positive that Jason Hale is dealing in drugs?'

'Maggie, I've told you, the evidence all points in his direction. In fact, something's afoot because the courier's been seen more frequently at his factory.'

'But couldn't it be someone other than Jason? Someone who works in the factory?'

'The stuff is coming from Singapore, we're pretty sure of that. And he's there almost half the time.'

'Could you find out? Have Customs look through a shipment?'

'And blow our plans up?' Oliver's voice was stern. 'Maggie, I plan to get everyone in this ring from the kingpin on down to the lowliest pusher. I don't want Hale to get suspicious. He hasn't caught on to you, has he?'

No, Maggie thought miserably, not precisely. 'He doesn't have a clue about me.'

'Good. Now, is there any news?'

'Not much. . . .' and she hesitated and Oliver said, 'Yes?'

'Well, I heard Jason and Theodore discussing an employee called Sam, I didn't catch the last name. He retired while Jason was gone and now he can't be found.'

'Could be interesting, I'll have the men look into it. Anything else?'

'No—well, yes. I had a small talk with Theodore about Hale Enterprises. He got very nervous when I mentioned the expansion.'

'Nervous? In what way?'

'Nothing I could put my finger on, but I could tell that talking about it made him uncomfortable. He's adamantly opposed to having Jason expand the business.'

'Hmmm,' Oliver said in a speculative tone. 'I wonder why Wolf objects. Unless he knows that Jason doesn't have the cash.'

'But he would, wouldn't he?' Maggie said quickly. 'If Jason is, as you say, dealing in heroin, he must be rolling in money.'

'You're right,' Oliver said slowly. 'It doesn't make sense.'

'Maybe you've got it wrong,' Maggie said hopefully. 'Maybe Jason isn't the man that. . . .'

'Maggie, don't overdo the flights of fancy. It's my job

to worry about the angles, and it's yours to be my eyes and ears. Just be careful and don't let Hale con you, understand?'

Maggie swallowed. 'Yes.'

'He isn't what he seems to be. I've heard he's good-looking and charming and has a way with women, but don't let that façade fool you. Just remember what he's involved in, okay?'

Maggie stared bleakly out at the parking lot of Merrick's gas station where two rusting cars and a delapidated truck sat in decaying splendour. 'Okay,' she said. 'I'll remember.'

# CHAPTER FIVE

DAVID MOSS arrived at Dragon's Point the very next afternoon. His arrival was marked by the screech of brakes, a rush of birds into the nearby trees and the loud and raucous sound of his car radio playing hard rock. The music was such a jarring sound that Maggie was jolted out of the book she was reading, her eyes widening at the blast of drums and heavy beat. By common consent, no one played a radio at Dragon's Point; it was disruptive, an intrusion of the outside world into an environment whose only sounds were those of the lake, the wildlife and the piano crescendos of Jason's classical pieces. The sudden blare of music made her teeth set on edge, a reaction she was to have during the rest of David's stay, a four-day period when the stresses and strains that existed below the surface of life at Dragon's Point threatened to break the fragile and superficially smooth surface of their existence.

David Moss was everything Maggie had imagined him to be—only worse. He was a tall, thin man of about thirty-five with blond good looks that were slightly the worse for wear. His clothes were a bit too flashy, he smiled a bit too brilliantly, and his heartiness was just the slightest shade this side of overdone. There was something about him that smacked of phoniness. His teeth seemed to be too white, Maggie would have sworn that he dyed his hair, and the ring on his little finger had to be too big to be a real diamond. When he got out of his car on the day of his arrival, she hadn't been able to see what his eyes were like. They were shaded by sunglasses, the kind that are metallic and glittery, shielding the eyes behind them and reflecting, in distorted shapes, the world in front.

92

'Hey, babe,' he had said as Carley ran out the back door and threw herself into his arms, 'it's long time, no see.'

'And I'll bet you've been up to no good,' Carley said, laughing up at him. 'I didn't think you were going to make it.'

David had disengaged himself from her arms and put up his hands in mock self-defence. 'Hey, babe,' two words, Maggie presumed, that prefaced everything he said, 'when David Moss says he's coming, he doesn't go back on his word.'

Carley linked her arm through his and pulled him over to Maggie. 'Come and meet Maggie. I told you about her, we were best friends in college. Maggie, this is David.'

Maggie saw the plea of entreaty in Carley's brown eyes and stretched out her hand. 'Hello,' she said with a smile, 'I'm glad to meet you.'

'Hey, babe,' David had said enthusiastically, not noticing Maggie's sudden wince as he took off his sunglasses and surveyed her with his pale blue eyes, 'it's a pleasure.' And he had taken her hand into his soft one and pumped it up and down.

David seemed to be ill at ease at Dragon's Point, and Maggie couldn't decide what had made him come. He didn't want to fish; in fact, he didn't seem to know one end of a fishing pole from the other. He didn't swim; he didn't care about sunbathing, and he had absolutely no interest in walks around the lake. He spent most of his time sitting on one of the porches, drinking beer and talking, in an undertone, to Carley. They sat huddled together, laughing or whispering. Their behaviour made Maggie feel distinctly uncomfortable, and she knew she wasn't the only one who felt that way. Theodore kept out of their way, and she could tell that Jason was smouldering beneath his overly polite façade as genial host. David rubbed him the wrong way, and Maggie could see it by the hostile glint in his eye, the clenching

of his jaw and the way he disappeared early in the
morning to go fishing and didn't return until after
dinner every night.

Carley knew that David didn't fit in at Dragon's Point,
and Maggie had caught her throwing a defiant glance at
Jason's receding back, but she acted as if she didn't care.
She was gracious enough to try to include Maggie in their
conversations, but Maggie was not able to follow their
gossip. She did not know the acquaintances that they
shared in common, had not attended the legendary wild
parties they laughed about and could not have cared less
about who was sleeping with whom. So she tried to keep
clear of them whenever she could, going for long walks by
herself or taking a book down on to the beach while she
sunbathed. She missed Carley's company and looked
forward to David's departure. And she was utterly
thankful that, in one respect, Carley had the decency to
behave correctly. If David and Carley were sleeping
together, it was not obvious to anyone at Dragon's Point.
As far as Maggie knew, they went to separate bedrooms
at night and stayed there.

It was curious, Maggie thought, as she passed the
porch down on her way to the beach one afternoon and
saw their two heads together. She couldn't imagine
what the relationship was between David and Carley.
Although they were physically affectionate with one
another, she would have sworn that there was a decided
lack of sexual interest between them. She might have
called their connection to one another friendship except
that there was an uneven substance to it. Carley hung
on David with a fawning servility that Maggie had
never witnessed before. She jumped up to light his
cigarettes; she laughed at his bad jokes; she acted as if
he were the master and she were the slave. It was a
peculiar relationship, and Maggie couldn't make heads
or tails out of it. She only knew that Carley's behaviour
made her feel slightly sick and that she was happier
lying on the beach where she couldn't see it or hear it.

Being left to her own devices was, unfortunately, one of the worst things that could have happened to Maggie at this point. The truth was that she was miserable about herself and about Jason. She couldn't put that kiss on the beach out of her mind and the memory of her own tears appalled her. She wasn't a weeper; she never cried, never—not when her mother had left home, not when the kids at her high school had ignored her or, even worse, taunted her, not even when Nicholas had made his devastating farewell. She had learned early in life how to put on a mask, how to shield her emotions from the prying eyes of others, how to maintain dry eyes in the face of adversity and emotional situations that would have had other women in tears. Maggie had always been proud of her stoicism; she had been able to count on it to get her through difficult times. She had never lost her poise or her composure until she and Jason had kissed on the beach. Then she had come flying apart as if she were made of glass, and the knowledge that she was fragile and vulnerable left her feeling helpless.

She hadn't known that she was going to cry. She had been enjoying the sensations of the afternoon to the point that she had forgotten who she was, who Jason was. She had loved the feel of Jason's mouth moving against hers, his hands stroking her body, the heat he had radiated against her, the slow, delicious and persistent beat of her own desire. Maggie hadn't felt that way in a long time, not since the first time that Nicholas had taken her to bed, and she had revelled in the luxurious timelessness of passion, the suspended moments when nothing mattered except the meeting of two bodies, each separate and yet uniquely qualified to fit together. The hot tide of lovemaking had carried her with its impetuous force until Hercules had intervened. Maggie had laughed then; she couldn't help it, but her laughter had merely been the flip side of her tears. They had appeared without warning, springing into her eyes, causing her to bend her head to hide the horror of exposure. When Jason had called her name, she had looked at him through a misty veil and seen the shock on his face. She had scrambled to her feet then, clutching the towel in front of her, gripped by the urgent desire to escape.

She couldn't imagine what Jason must think of her; her cheeks flamed with embarrassment when she remembered what she had done. It was one thing to fight the battle of attraction within, but quite another to let it show on the surface with capitulation, tears and then flight. The moment that the erotic spell had been broken, Maggie had heard Oliver's voice in her head and misery had taken over. The tears were symbolic of her confusion and unhappiness. She wanted Jason; she wanted to go to bed with him. It was even possible, although she fought this one, that she was just the slightest bit in love with him. She felt an enchantment whenever they were together, the air shimmered with anticipation and excitement. But Maggie didn't want to love Jason, feel attracted to him or even like him. She wanted to hate him; she wished desperately that she found him repulsive and ugly, but she didn't. Unfortunately, she didn't.

When Maggie had talked Oliver into letting her be an informer, she had only thought of the thrill of suspense and the fun of it. She had envisioned herself as some kind of female James Bond; suave, nonchalant, unafraid, glamorous. Not that she had really expected to confront danger. Although Oliver had been deadly serious, she had been incapable of seeing the situation at Dragon's Point as other than trivial. She had thought that working for the RCMP would be a lark, a fling, an event she would laugh about later with friends or use as an amusing subject at a cocktail party. She saw herself with a crowd of people, holding a glass in her hands and laughing lightly—'I'll never forget the time I was a narc for the. . . .' But it hadn't turned out to be amusing at all. Maggie was now held in a bind so restrictive that she couldn't break free. No matter which way she turned and struggled, she was caught between a fatal attraction for Jason and the knowledge that he was probably Oliver's hated drug-trafficker.

Maggie sighed as she placed her towel on the flat rock that overlooked the lake and lay down on it, her back exposed to the warm rays of the sun. She tried to let her mind ease into that non-thinking, neutral blankness that comes with the heat and inactivity of sunbathing, but it wasn't easy to forget the path her life had taken and its tangle of messy emotional underbrush. Not even the sun beating on her head could burn that growth of suspicion, unhappiness and misery back, leaving her once again with the clean purity that had come before. The seeds of self-doubt had been sown and she was reaping its harvest; a cornucopia of tears and the unwelcome knowledge that even Maggie Jordan, resilient, tough and hard, could break.

'Let's dance!' Carley exclaimed the next night as she stepped down into the living room and tossed a sweater on to a nearby chair. 'We've been so dull lately.'

Her look of impatience took in the living room and its occupants, and Maggie had to agree that by most standards, they were pretty dull. She, Jason and Theodore were occupying separate parts of the room, their noses buried in their respective books. There hadn't been a sound made for the past half-hour except for the flipping of pages, the steady ticking of the clock and the night noises that came through the screened patio door; the chirping song of crickets, the occasional lonely hooting of an owl. It was a quiet evening which had been the culmination of a quiet day. Maggie, who hadn't been sleeping well, had napped during the afternoon, Jason had been on yet another fishing expedition, Theodore had closeted himself in the den to make phone calls. For people like Carley and David who thrived on an exciting nightlife, Dragon's Point left a lot to be desired.

'Not me,' said Theodore, rising from a chair and closing his book. 'I'm too old for that sort of thing.'

'Theo, you're never too old to dance.' Carley stepped lightly down into the living room. 'The records are over there,' she added to David who had followed her in.

'My dear,' said Theo, 'I may not be too old to dance, but I've reached that age when looking ridiculous has lost its charm. But don't let me stop you. I can read in my room.'

Carley's pout was short-lived. By the time Theo had left the living room, she had snapped off most of the lights so that the room was only semi-lit and she was standing in the middle of it, her arms spread wide, twirling around and around. A short blue skirt swirled around her legs; her shoulders in the blue tank top were bare and gleamed a pale gold. Maggie thought that Carley looked like a spirite. Her bare feet drummed a rhythm into the carpet and her blonde hair glittered and swung in the light. 'Put something jazzy on, David, something with a good beat.' She made a face at Jason. 'And nothing that sounds like Chopin.'

Jason slowly put down his book. 'I thought you liked classical music.'

Carley danced over to him, her feet keeping an imaginary beat, and put out her hands. 'I do, dear Uncle, but I need a change. Come on, dance with me.' When Jason looked hesitant, she tilted her head to one side with that appraising glance. 'Or would you rather go join Theo and do crossword puzzles?'

'Dear niece,' Jason said with a light sarcasm, 'I'm not six feet under yet.'

Carley reached down and tugged at Jason's hands. 'Come on, Uncle, prove it.' And Jason rose reluctantly from his seat, a tall figure in dark jeans and a blue shirt that was opened at the collar.

David had put on a rock record with a quick, finger-snapping beat that drowned out the sounds of the lake and made the light from the lamps seem glittery. The room had almost instantaneously taken on the air of a discotheque. Carley's feet moved so quickly that they were a blur; Jason swayed and bent with the rhythm. They looked good together and Maggie smiled as she watched them. The truce between uncle and niece had been an uneasy one. There had not been any arguments since the spat on the first night of Jason's stay, but neither had there been any accord. An unspoken pact had held them at arm's length. Now, she saw Jason laugh at something Carley said to him, and she hoped that was indication that the wariness between them had eased. Certainly, Carley was doing her best to be charming. She was smiling, her eyes sparkled with amusement, she was happy. For the first time since she had arrived at Dragon's Point, Maggie recognised the old Carley—the girl who had seized on to life with such enthusiasm and verve.

'Hey, babe. How about a dance?'

'Oh, I. . . .'

But David was pulling her up out of her chair and down into the conversation pit where Carley and Jason were dancing. The music had now altered to a song with a slow, sensual beat, and he put one arm around her waist, tucking one of her hands against his chest and pulling her so close to him that her face was against his shoulder. He hummed to the music, seemingly oblivious to Maggie's unhappy acquiescence. For all his thinness, David was surprisingly muscular. She couldn't budge and her head was locked into position. She could hear the steady drumming of his heart in her left ear, and it mixed oddly with his voice.

'*Ta*, te, dum, *ta*, te, dum. Hey, babe, what do you do for kicks?'

'I go out and buy a terrific pair of shoes with sharp toes,' she said coldly.

David looked down at her in bewilderment, his pale blue eyes confused. 'Hey,' he said, 'no insult. You just don't seem to be getting any joy out of life.'

Now, there was an oddly perceptive remark, Maggie thought wryly. Who would have ever thought that it would come out of someone as seemingly obtuse and self-centred as David Moss? 'I'm doing fine,' she said.

'Hey, babe, I'm not criticising you, but I hate to see a good-looking woman wasting her time. You live in Toronto?'

'No, Ottawa.'

'Now, that's a shame. I could show you a good time in Toronto.'

Maggie wondered if this was a pass, David Moss-style. 'I'm not the partying type.'

David shrugged. 'There are other ways to have fun.'

It sounded like a pass to Maggie, but it didn't feel like one. There wasn't even the slightest hint of sexuality in it. 'Such as?' she asked.

'Hey, babe,' David said with an exaggerated drawl, 'I don't give out my secrets for nothing.'

Maggie wondered whether she was being stupid or whether David was speaking in riddles. She hadn't a clue what he was talking about, but rather than push it, she changed the subject. 'Have you known Carley for long?'

'About a year.'

'Since the divorce?'

'A bit before that. She's a great kid, she really is.' He tried to pull her back into his arms again, but Maggie resisted. She wanted to get to the bottom of Carley's relationship to David if she could.

'You go out with her a lot?'

'We're pals, we party together. Carley likes to have a good time. She was in the dumps when I got here, but look at her now. She's living it up.'

There was something to his claim. Since David had arrived, Carley had perked up, her laughter coming easily, her gestures careless and happy. Even now, as she danced with Jason, Maggie could see how Carley was throwing herself into the enjoyment of the moment. Her past cares seemed to have been shed with the onset of the music, the soft lights, the chance to merge with an insistent and wholly physical rhythmical beat.

'Did you know her husband?' she asked David.

His pale blue eyes blinked, and then the smile with the teeth whiter than white broke out again. 'I missed that pleasure.'

'Do you think Carley's got over her marriage?'

He shrugged again. 'Hey, babe, I'm not a shrink.'

'No, but. . . .' Maggie's voice died away in confusion, and she silently let David take over the dancing once more, his hand on her waist pressing her close to him. She couldn't figure any of it out; she felt as if she were caught in a maze that was composed of passages that didn't lead anywhere and doors that opened in the wrong direction. While it couldn't be denied that David's arrival at Dragon's Point had perked Carley up immensely, Maggie had no idea what held the two of them together. David was phony, shallow and not particularly intelligent. He had a vocabulary limited to slang expressions, and he seemed to have no interest in anything other than rock music, beer and parties. And, while he was good-looking in a way, Maggie felt nothing towards him but a faint revulsion. His hair was too blond, his eyes too pale, that smile as artificial as that in a child's drawing.

Yet, something had to hold Carley to him, something that went far deeper than the surface. Maggie thought of the way Carley had served David lunch, fussing over him, afraid that he wouldn't like what she had made. There had been a hint of desperation to her actions. Maggie sensed the tie between them, but she didn't know what formed it. Not sex; at least, she didn't think so, and it certainly wasn't the brilliance of David's conversation. But there was a connection, a strong one, that lay below the surface. Maggie would have given her eye teeth to know what it was.

'Change partners!' Carley announced and, dancing over to David, pulled him next to her. Much as Maggie had not wanted to dance with David, she was now extremely reluctant to give up the sudden protection of his arms. She didn't want to dance with Jason; she didn't want to get that close to him, but she had little choice. 'And Maggie dances with Jason,' Carley announced gaily, pushing Jason in Maggie's direction. 'Come on, you two. The night's still young.'

Maggie turned to Jason and, for a second, their eyes locked, their communication silent beneath Carley's laughter and the steady beat of the music. Then his gaze left hers and took a slow tour down her body; from the middle parting in her chestnut hair to the slender curve of her shoulders, across the fullness of her breasts stretching the fabric of her plaid shirt to the trim circle of her waist, down the span of her hips in tight denim to the high arch of her bare foot. It was a thorough examination, it felt like a striptease. By the time Jason had completed that leisurely downward glance, Maggie's nerve endings were on fire. He had let her know precisely what he was remembering, and that knowledge made her burn. When he pulled her close to him, she had to forcibly keep herself from flinching; she didn't want him to know that everywhere he touched her, a spark flared on her skin.

'Imagine,' he murmured in an ironical tone, 'having you in my arms once again and no Hercules in sight.'

'I like that dog,' she said, trying to keep her voice light.

'Since when?'

'Since he developed such a great sense of timing.'

'I've been talking to him about that.'

'Have you?'

'It seems that he was feeling a little bit jealous, you know, a bit down in the mouth about all the attention he wasn't getting. I've been neglecting Herc a bit; at least, that's how he sees it.'

'Herc needs a girlfriend.'

Jason shook his head mournfully. 'I've tried,' he said. 'God knows how I've tried to get that dog interested in women.'

Maggie smiled and let Jason pull her closer to him. So this was how it was going to be, she thought; light, flirtatious, non-threatening. Neither she nor Jason had said much to one another after that episode on the beach and, since he'd taken to disappearing when David was around, their paths barely crossed. At first, she had sensed that he was angry; those golden-green eyes had seemed particularly stormy whenever they glanced in her direction, but that emotion had given way to curiosity and speculation. Maggie intrigued Jason, she knew that, but she wasn't under any illusions as to the reasons why. As Carley had pointed out earlier, Jason Hale wasn't used to challenges when it came to women, and Maggie was proving to be very difficult. She could tell that she was a thorn in Jason's side, a conundrum that refused to be solved, a puzzle that wouldn't fit together. When a man was accustomed to bowling women over like so many ten-pins, the one that trembled and wavered but still remained standing was bound to be a target.

Still, he was very clever and very nonchalant. No one would have ever guessed by his conversation or the way he was holding her that Jason had once held Maggie almost nude in his arms, their bodies aroused to fever pitch, their skin meeting in the flushed heat of lovemaking. He was now treating Maggie as if he had gone two steps backward to square one, as if they were at the start of a flirtation that could lead to an affair instead of being caught in the middle of one that refused to be consummated. Nothing at all was said of what had transpired between them; the atmosphere was easy, and Maggie slowly relaxed and let Jason's arm wind around her waist, allowing the music to filter into her consciousness and the feel of that hard body next to hers lull her into the light haze of a sensual trance.

'Do you know what I'd like to be?' Jason asked.

Maggie smiled up at him. 'What?'

'The hero in a romance novel.'

'Why?'

'They always get the girl in the end.'

'But,' she pointed out, 'the girl always gets the hero, too. They marry one another.'

'You don't think I'm interested in marriage?'

'You've managed to miss it so far.'

'It isn't easy finding a wife.'

'Advertise.'

'Advertise? You mean in the papers?'

Maggie shrugged. 'Sure. "Eligible male, thirty-five years of age, healthy and with adequate income, seeks woman for permanent, matrimonial relationship."'

'Boring,' he said. 'I'd never answer that.'

'Well, what would you say?'

'Let's see. "Handsome, charming male with dark hair and fascinating green eyes . . .".'

'Does your back hurt?'

His eyebrow arched. 'My back?'

'From patting yourself so often.'

Jason gave her a grin and went on, '". . . seeks a woman who likes chilled white wine, whirlpool baths, candlelight, beach scenes, back rubs,"' at this Maggie had the grace to blush, '"and Samoyeds. Admiration, adoration and adulation available for a woman with wit, laughter and a hint of mystery."' He paused, thinking, and then added, '"For chance encounters of a matrimonial kind. All responses will be answered." There, how's that?'

'No doubt you'll be deluged,' she said drily.

'Tempted to answer.'

Maggie shook her head.

'Not interested in marriage?'

Maggie gave Jason a wide-eyed, innocent look. 'Is this a back-handed proposal?'

Jason shook his head reprovingly. 'No answering questions with questions.'

'I'm not interested in marriage.'

'Now, that's different,' Jason said. 'I don't think I've ever met a woman who wasn't interested in marriage.'

'Even a man of experience can stumble sometimes.'

'Ouch,' Jason said with a wince. 'And to what can we attribute your reluctance to be found in the marital state, Miss Jordan?'

The look she gave him was level. 'I don't want to be dominated.'

'Did Nicholas dominate you?'

'Nicholas who?'

A smile lurked in the corners of Jason's mouth. Talking to Maggie was like aiming at a swiftly moving target. Their repartee snapped and sizzled like a whip cracked in the air, its direction shifting and switching, turning and twisting, all within seconds. He had never met a woman who had Maggie's conversational skills; he'd never talked to a woman whose words could lead him on a merry chase through angled paths, around unsuspected corners and down unbelievably inclined slopes.

'An odd name,' he said.

'Odd?'

'Nicholas Who.'

Maggie couldn't prevent her laughter. 'Sort of like John Doe,' she said.

'Yes,' Jason agreed solemnly, 'it has that ring of nonentity. But let's get back to marriage. I'm very interested in the institution.'

'It's mundane,' she said. 'Toast and eggs, electrical bills, house insurance. . . .'

'Companionship, a shared bed, regular sex.'

'I would have thought a man of your type would find that rather boring.'

'And you? Would you find it boring?'

As he had suspected, Maggie didn't like that question. 'Hasn't the weather been lovely?'

But Jason was not to be deterred. 'Of course, I think your feelings about sex are directly related to your mother's leaving.'

Maggie couldn't help it; she stiffened in his arms. 'I dislike amateur psychologists.'

'Really?'

'Really, Mr Hale.'

The music had altered now to another rhythm, a faster one. Its beat demanded that they step apart, move in mirror images to one another, their bodies close and yet not touching. Over the insistent music, Maggie heard Carley's voice and her shout of laughter. It had a frenetic, wild sound to it as if Carley's happiness had slipped, and she was trying desperately hard to clamber back up to where she had been. Maggie glanced at the other couple who were gyrating to the music. Jason's gaze followed hers and then inexorably returned to rest on Maggie's face once again. Her colour was high, the freckles visible on her tanned cheeks, and her hair swung on her shoulders, a mass of chestnut curls.

'Why,' he asked, 'don't you like to talk about yourself?'

Maggie immediately bristled, and the blue eyes glared at him. 'I don't,' she said coldly, 'like invasions of my privacy.'

Jason was enough of a debater to know an irrelevant obstacle when he saw one. 'I think your attitude towards sex is a subject of mutual interest.'

Maggie stopped dancing. 'Well, I don't.'

'Afraid?' he jeered softly.

Maggie's chin could have done a duchess proud. 'Afraid!' Of what?'

His voice was too low to be heard by the others, but quite loud enough to reach Maggie's ears. 'Of sex, darling. That's been obvious all along.'

Maggie stomped out of the living room after that, marched into her room, slammed the door behind her and slumped down on her bed, cursing Jason Hale with every colourful word in her vocabulary. She hated him; it was as simple as that. She hated him for needling her, for poking at her, for trying to pry secrets from her that had been buried so deeply that Maggie had found them easy to ignore. Life was much easier, she thought as she stared out of her darkened window, when it was unexamined and left to its own devices. One could skate on the surface then, blithely ignorant of the cracks below, the dangerous crevasses in one's psyche. But when one was forced to stop and look down into those dark voids, then life grew difficult, complicated and unpleasant.

Despite the fact that Jason had no real idea of the overt reason why she had held him off, he had perceived, with deadly accuracy, her underlying motives. He had seen right into her heart, and that was one place that Maggie kept under lock and key. And he hadn't only done it tonight. There had been those words murmured on the beach when she had been too mesmerised by the sun and his touch to think deeply about the things he had said. Later, when she had remembered them, Maggie had shut them away. She hadn't wanted to think about sex with Nicholas or the way her mother's leaving might have affected her own feelings of sexuality. It was far safer to ignore such thoughts and let them slip, once more, back into their dark oblivion. She hated Jason for dragging them out again into the open where they could taunt her and make her miserable.

It was true that sex with Nicholas had been a failure; Jason had been so right about that. She'd been such a damn fool although, when it first began, Maggie hadn't thought that an affair with Nicholas would be anything but glorious. She had fallen head over heels in love with him; she had thought the sun set at his feet and rose over his head. In all her earlier dealings with the opposite sex, Maggie had been cautious, circumspect and cool. With Nicholas, she had thrown aside her fears, believing that his passion for her must equal her own for him. And when the glittering tower of her illusions had crumbled and crashed, cut cruelly apart by the whiplike effect of Nicholas' words, Maggie's sexual self had retreated back into its protective shell. She had dated; she'd made no attempt to hide her femininity or her good looks, but no man had marred the cool surface of her emotions again—not until Jason.

When she looked back on her affair with Nicholas, Maggie could see just how dazzled she had been. She had met Nicholas at a party and his wit and good looks had intrigued her from the first. He had a confidence that commanded respect, a lazy smile that was sexual in the extreme and an eye for pretty women. Although he was only in his early thirties, Nicholas had been the golden boy of the federal bureaucracy, moving from department to department, position to higher position, until he was close to the seat of power. He had vast quantities of charm that concealed an underlying ambition and ruthlessness. And, while he was the first man that Maggie had ever gone to bed with, she'd been well aware that she wasn't Nicholas' first lover by any means. He had let her know by innuendo, reference and remark that there had been many others before her. But she had been too blinded by infatuation to consider that Nicholas would treat her in the same cavalier manner that he'd treated those other women. She had thought she would be special, different, unique. It had hurt; it had hurt like hell to discover that she wasn't.

She'd had a sickening, *déjà vu* feeling when Jason had spoken about his vast horde of unnamed and faceless women, but when he had ruefully admitted that he was thankful he was beyond the stage of indiscriminate promiscuity, she had realised that he was not like Nicholas at all. Nicholas had never developed either kindness or sensitivity. She had come to him with her sexual barriers down, her body ready and aroused, desire softening her until she had thought she would melt with its heat. And he had as effectively destroyed her passion as if he had taken a hammer to it and beaten it into a small, wasted lump. For a long time, Maggie had believed that their failure in bed had been her fault. How could Nicholas, with all his vaunted sexual experience, leave her feeling so empty and unsatisfied?

What Maggie remembered most from the aftermath of her affair with Nicholas had been the urgent feeling that she must be in control once again. She had let everything go for Nicholas—her job, the house, her friends; she needed to organise her life, put her affairs in order, seek a calm perspective. And with an energy she hadn't known she possessed, Maggie had pulled herself together. Within weeks of her break-up with Nicholas, no one would have guessed that she had thought she would die of a broken heart and a badly bruised ego. And her wariness of sexual impulse ran deep. Subconsciously, she had aligned herself with her mother, a woman who had run away from her husband, who had thrown away a home and a family, who had lost all *control* for another man's bed. While Maggie might consciously admit that Sandra and Daniel Jordan must have been incompatible in a thousand ways, and it was more than likely that Daniel was the sort of man who should never have married in the first place, underneath she believed something far different. Her rational sympathy for Sandra was underlain by an irrational and highly emotional sense of betrayal. Many women left their husbands, but how many mothers, willingly and happily, left their daughters?

It had taken Jason to point out the connection beneath her own sexual feelings and her mother's leaving. Yes, Maggie thought, she *was* frightened of sex. She had never been able to believe that Sandra hadn't loved her or, at the very least, hadn't reluctantly left her behind. It had been far easier to think of sex as a wild beast, a hungry and cruel tormentor that had forced Sandra to abandon her for the embraces of a stranger. Even at the tender and innocent age of ten, Maggie had dimly made this connection, not realising how she had gripped on to this explanation in order to make her mother's leaving tolerable. For years, she had day-dreamed of Sandra coming home, of their meeting, arms around one another, of the faintly remembered sweet scent of crushed roses, of her mother whispering the long-awaited words, 'I love you, Maggie. I missed you so much.'

Maggie had fought any indication that she could be like her mother, and now she desperately sought ways to remain in command of emotions and desires that threatened to break loose, to shatter her poise, to send her into the chaotic region of uncertainty. Yet, she felt as if she were waging a losing war against her attraction to Jason. When she had succumbed to him on the beach, she had cried, yes, for that overwhelming barrier that Oliver had set up between Jason and herself. But she had also cried for the knowledge of her vulnerability, for her dizzying, reckless spin into passion and, she now understood, for the battle that was being waged so deeply in her psyche. The ravenous dragon of sex lay within, ready to clench her in its grasping claws and swallow her whole.

# CHAPTER SIX

MAGGIE found the pills two days after David's departure. She had gone into Carley's room, looking for a borrowed book, when she inadvertently came upon a large jar filled with pills and tablets of every shade of the rainbow, pink, pale green, bright red, orange, lemon yellow. She picked it up from its nesting place in Carley's dresser and stared at it, both horrified and suddenly understanding. She'd been quite naive, Maggie now realised, not to have guessed, not to have even suspected that Carley was taking drugs.

The evidence had always been there had she been aware enough to see it. There had been Carley's erratic behaviour, her thinness, her desperate dependence on David Moss, that euphoric high she'd had the night they'd danced and now the bouts of heavy sleeping, and the occasionally slurred speech when she woke up. Maggie had attributed all of Carley's actions to depression, to emotional instability, to grief. She had even believed that Jason was being too hard on Carley to insist that she go back to work and snap out of it. She had thought that grief and sadness must take their proper course before they could be properly exorcised. She had counselled Jason on patience and perserverance, and he had uneasily agreed with her. In her blindness and ignorance, she had never once considered the possibility that Carley took pills. She even recognised some of them from the course she had taken under Oliver's supervision. There were uppers in the jar, stimulants to give Carley a false sense of happiness, and downers, the barbituates that would make Carley sleep when the night seemed too long or when the uppers made her jittery. They were pills, Maggie knew, that were beneficial when used properly and addictive when abused. And their use could lead to a desire for stronger and more dangerous drugs; speed, coke and dope.

She turned slowly when Carley walked into the bedroom and the other woman stopped in her tracks, her glance going from Maggie's face to the incriminating jar in her hands. Carley's mouth turned down, throwing the lines between her nose and lips into sharp relief. She looked older than her twenty-seven years then, pale beneath her tan, dark circles beneath her eyes, the gold of her hair dulled to a pale ash. Then she shrugged and sat down on her bed.

'Now, you know,' she said.

'I wasn't snooping. I was looking for that novel you borrowed yesterday.'

'You were bound to find out eventually. I didn't think I could keep it a secret for ever.'

'Is it David who supplies you with these things?' Maggie asked as she glanced down at the jar with revulsion.

'Yes.'

'He's not your boyfriend at all, is he?'

'No, he's my source, I guess you would say,' Carley's mouth twisted. 'My own personal pusher.'

'Do you know how dangerous these things are?'

Carley looked down at her hands where the fingers were entwined together, her knuckles turning white. 'Don't preach to me, Maggie. I don't want to hear it.'

There was so much tension in Carley's body that Maggie could see it. Her thin shoulders were rigid, the muscles were knotted in her forearms, her knees bare beneath her skirt were pressed so tightly together that the sound of bone on bone was audible. Maggie's initial sense of horror receded and she felt an overwhelming rush of sympathy. She sat down next to Carley on the bed and put her hand gently over those taut fingers.

'I don't mean to preach,' she said. 'I won't make any

value judgments on you; I'm just afraid that you're hurting yourself. How long has this been going on?'

'For about a year.'

'Was it David who . . .?'

'Don't blame him. It was my doctor who started me on tranquillisers for depression. I just found that he wouldn't prescribe enough for me so I started to ask around and found that David could get his hands on an unlimited supply.'

'How?'

'I don't know how he does it, Maggie. I don't want to ask.'

'Have you tried to stop?'

Carley's shoulders slumped in unhappiness. 'Sure I have. I tried when I first came here, but I couldn't sleep at night and I felt so jittery. I was down to only a few pills; that's why David came.'

'You're not sleeping with David at all, are you?'

For the first time, a glint of humour came into Carley's eyes. 'God, no. I don't even think David likes women that way. We have a very utilitarian relationship. David keeps me in pills and escorts me around, and I give him money. It's been very satisfactory.'

A very twisted relationship, Maggie thought, and one that kept Carley in a vicious circle of dependency. She could just see how David's constant company had led Carley into a bad crowd, kept her in social circles where she wouldn't meet decent friends and had held other men at arm's length so that there was no chance that she would ever attract the interest of a nice man. Not that she blamed David entirely for what had happened to Carley. She sensed that Carley was afraid of getting out in the real world again, of trying to hold down a job, of finding an eligible man. David was her shield and her protection against the difficult responsibilities of leading a normal life.

Maggie gently pulled Carley's hands apart so that she could hold one of them between hers. 'I hate to see you like this,' she said softly. 'You're hurting your health and your mind and. . . .'

The hand was yanked out of hers and Carley, standing up with an impatient gesture, walked over to the window and stared out of it. 'I know all the platitudes and cliches,' she said, her teeth gritted together, 'and I feel enough self-pity so that I don't need yours.'

'Taking drugs is destructive,' Maggie began, 'and. . . .'

Carley whirled around. 'Do you think I don't know it?' she asked angrily. 'Do you think I'm so dumb that I don't know what I'm doing to myself? But you don't know the alternatives, Maggie, you don't know what it's like to have thoughts so bad and so horrifying that the only way to silence them is with drugs.'

'Did you ever try counselling or. . . .'

'Who the hell did you think started me on tranquillisers? My shrink, that's who!'

Carley's rage and vehemence shocked Maggie. She stood up, her hands outstretched. 'Carley, I didn't intend to put you down.'

But Carley ignored her. 'It's so easy for other people to judge, to give advice, to tell me what to do. They haven't any idea what my life's like; they don't know what the nights are like, those long, horrible nights when there's nothing but the darkness and my mind spinning and turning like a wheel that won't stop. I feel like I'm going crazy then. Crazy!'

'You're not crazy,' Maggie protested.

Anger flushed Carley's cheeks. 'How do you know?' she demanded. 'Maggie, you don't have the slightest inkling what it's like. You're strong and tough; you've always been that way. Life doesn't hit you the same way as it hits me; you take things in your stride. You know how to cope. I never have. Never. My parents swathed me in lamb's wool you took care of me in college, I walked right into Alex's arms. But when my marriage was over there was no one, and suddenly I was on my own.' Tears sprang into her eyes, and Carley quickly turned away and stared out the window again. 'It was devastating to discover that there was nothing there, Maggie. When all my buffers were gone, there was nothing left.'

There was a small silence in the room as Maggie tried to understand what Carley was saying. She knew that Carley, as a child, had been highly protected and spoiled beyond reason. What had saved her from being obnoxious as an adolescent and young woman had been her high spirits and sense of humour. It was true that she had believed, implicitly, that the world owed her a living, but that belief had been secondary to an exuberant enthusiasm for life. When they had been together in college, Maggie had been so taken with Carley's effervescence that she had failed to understand something very basic about the other girl's personality: Carley had no firm sense of her own identity; she had used other people in a desperate attempt to define herself. Maggie could remember how clinging Carley had been and, sometimes, how demanding. She had needed Maggie's admiration and affection, just as she had needed her parent's adoration and a husband's love. She had used all the people in her life as mirrors in which she could see her reflection; as beloved daughter, as Maggie's best friend, as Alex's wife. Without those definitions, she was lost.

'And because there was nothing,' Carley went on in a low voice, 'I looked for something to fill the gap. Jason wanted me to work for him, he would have gladly stepped in and taken control of my life, but I was tired of being treated like a child again. I wanted to prove that I was someone, that I was an adult, that I could take care of myself. But it wasn't easy, you see. I needed things to help me, like analysis and drugs. I couldn't make it through a day without tranquillisers to dull the pain and the ... emptiness. It was then that I understood what losing the baby had really meant to me, Maggie.' Her voice faltered and then continued, 'And then I met David. Oh, I know he hangs around with me for my money, but he's fun. He knows how to have a good time. When I'm with him, I can forget who I am and what's happened to me.'

Maggie stared at Carley's back and saw how thin she was. The bones of her spine stood out as rocky bumps, the shoulder blades were sharp and angular. She wanted to put her arm around the other woman and hold her close as if, through an embrace, she could pass some of her own strength to that far too slender frame. But she knew better; every inch of Carley's rigid spine expressed a resistance to sympathy and pity. There was a pathetic sort of pride in the set of her shoulders; anger and frustration in the tightly clenched fists.

Perhaps if Carley had a goal, Maggie thought, something worth working for she would feel better about herself. 'You once had a great job. Couldn't you go back into television again?'

'My parents got that job for me,' Carley said bitterly. 'And ... I was afraid of it. I didn't think I could measure up. When Alex came along, I used him as an excuse to quit. You know, Maggie, money is an evil thing. I've always known that I didn't have to work and, as a result, I don't have an ambition worth discussing.'

Maggie felt a lump in her throat. 'Carley, you're a good person. I love you, I always have.'

Carley's head bent and her hands came up to her face. 'I ... I don't want your pity.'

'I know.'

Her voice was muffled in her hands. 'It's my life to ruin if I want.'

'But I'd like to help.'

'Oh, Maggie.' Carley's head lifted and her eyes were swimming with tears. 'I don't think there's anything you can do.'

Maggie came away from Carley's room with a frustrated and helpless feeling. There was no logic to the other woman's self-destructive tendencies, but she was well aware that logic rarely had a part in the type of emotional decisions that Carley was making. The need for escape from reality and her own misery was so strong that Carley was willing to lean on any crutch and seek any outlet, and her problems were so deep-seated and pervasive that Maggie's friendship wasn't adequate. It didn't matter how much sympathy and comfort she could offer Carley; none of it was enough.

It was partially this realisation that made Maggie approach Jason and, because she didn't want to talk to him about Carley in the vicinity of the cottage, she agreed to accompany him on a trip into the town beyond Merrick, a slightly larger metropolis called Fayetteville. She was apprehensive about the hours she would spend with him alone in the car, but she needn't have worried. All the way there, the conversation was light and inconsequential. Neither of them referred to the night they had danced together or his insinuations. They discussed the weather, the merits of a recent bestseller, the benefits of living in Toronto versus Ottawa and their mutual reluctance to go back to work in a week's time. The drive went quickly, and Maggie was surprised to find them entering Fayetteville, population 9,861.

'Is the shopping good?' Maggie asked as she got out of the car.

'You're going to be thrilled,' Jason said dryly.

Maggie discovered what he meant the minute she strolled down Fayetteville's only shopping district, Main Street. The town was one of those whose pretensions are small and whose offerings provided all the amenities of life, provided you weren't too particular. The grocery store sold the basics only, the drugstore's window was dusty and decorated with cut-glass bottles of perfume, and the dress shop, trying to encompass both practicality and fashion, had somehow missed the boat, the mannequins in the windows wearing styles that were several years out of date. Only the sports store seemed to have the vitality that was associated with city shopping. It was packed to the rafters with the latest equipment for boating, fishing and hunting and the aisles were filled with customers.

Jason and Maggie had separated for a couple of hours and done their respective shopping before meeting again at the car. Jason was waiting for her when she arrived, somewhat out of breath and weighed down with packages. He was leaning against the car, idly watching the passers-by, and Maggie was struck once again by just how distinctive looking Jason was. Perhaps she'd got used to him in the isolation of Dragon's Point; perhaps she had, with some success, put it out of her mind that he was one of the most attractive men she'd ever seen. But now it was brought forcibly home to her as she walked down the street towards him, catching him in an unconsciously sexy pose, one khaki-clad knee bent, a hand in his pocket stretching the fabric of his slacks over well-formed buttocks, broad shoulders twisted slightly sideways in royal blue, chiselled features caught in profile, the dark hair in a thick wave over one ear. He looked, Maggie thought, like a model from an ad in *Esquire*, impeccably dressed, fastidiously groomed and overwhelming in an entirely masculine way.

And the smile he gave her was breathtaking, the teeth straight and white, the glow of it lighting up those incredible golden-green eyes. 'It looks like you've done wonders for Fayetteville's economy,' he said as he took some of the bags out of her arms.

'Things are expensive up here,' Maggie said, pushing her hair out of her face. She had worn a sundress that day, a red cotton with blue piping on the bodice, blue sandals and a white straw hat with a circular brim. Every once in a while a breeze threatened to carry the hat away, and she was forced to put her hand on the top of her head to hold it in place.

'That's what happens,' Jason said, 'when a town lives on its tourists. They put the prices up in the summer and down in the winter.'

'And the selection,' Maggie said as she got in the car, 'is horrendous.'

Jason slid behind the wheel. 'City slicker,' he teased. The car's powerful engine came to life as he turned the key, and they moved slowly out into the sporadic traffic. For a while there was a silence in the car as Jason drove out of Fayetteville and on to the highway that led back to Dragon's Point. Then he glanced at her curiously and said, 'Cat got your tongue? I didn't think Maggie Jordan would ever let me get away with an insult.'

But Maggie didn't rise to the bait. She had decided to tell Jason about Carley's drug problem and had been waiting for the right moment to do so. It hadn't been an easy decision, but one she had debated over long and hard. At first, it had seemed to her that she might be betraying a confidence, but this line of thought had eventually yielded to the realisation that Carley's problem was so serious that she shouldn't keep it to herself. And there was no one else she could tell but Jason. He lived in Toronto, he had access to Carley's family, he would be there if she needed help. He was, she had finally realised, the logical person to confide in.

'I want to talk to you about Carley,' she said slowly.

'Oh?'

'She's on . . . drugs.'

He was silent then and Maggie looked over at him. He seemed to be concentrating on the road, his hands gripping the steering wheel. Now that they had left Fayetteville and its outskirts, they were back into uninhabited territory. The road, a slender two-way highway, dipped and turned, its grey surface shadowed by the trees that loomed on each side and the occasional outcropping of rock. The engine hummed, the clock on the dashboard ticked and the wind whistled against the car's acceleration.

'I wondered,' he finally said.

'Did you?'

'She's been acting oddly for a while. I asked her once, but she denied it. What's she on?'

'Uppers, downers, tranquillisers. David's supplying her with the stuff.'

'Bastard.'

The word was spoken in a low voice, and Maggie was surprised by the venom in it. She hadn't been able to guess what sort of response Jason would have to her news about Carley. In fact, telling him had been sort of an experiment—how would a man who deals in heroin take the news that his niece is addicted to drugs? Badly, it would seem, from the muscles that clenched in Jason's jaw and the grim line of his mouth.

'You can't really blame David,' Maggie said. 'He doesn't force the pills down her throat.'

'No, I know.'

'And Carley knows how destructive it is, but she says that she can't help herself. It's . . . so sad.'

'I've tried,' Jason said bleakly. 'I've tried so damn hard with Carley and I can't seem to get anywhere. She fights me off, she won't let me help. She could have worked for me and that would have filled her time, given her a chance to meet other people and kept her organised, but she refused. So I started taking her out with me to parties, to concerts, to any event I could think of, but she didn't want to be part of my world. I don't know why.'

'Maybe it frightened her,' Maggie said, 'maybe she thought she couldn't cope.'

Jason sighed. 'I don't have much family, Maggie. My parents are old and all that's left is my sister and Carley. Both sets of grandparents are dead and neither pair was very prolific. There's hardly any cousins and no small children. Maybe I'm old-fashioned, but I've always wanted to be part of a big family, a big, squabbling, raucous family.' The wistful sound in Jason's voice reminded Maggie of the time he had admitted the desire to be married. 'And Carley was always my idea of what a little sister would be like; tiny, blonde, charming, enchanting. We may be uncle and niece but there's only a thirteen-year difference, and I grew up feeling very protective of her. Hell, I even changed her diapers on occasion.'

Maggie chose her words carefully. 'I think Carley knows how you feel about her.'

'I doubt it,' Jason said, 'I think I overdid it. When I saw how unhappy she was, I nagged and kept at her until she balked.' He paused and then added with a faint trace of bitterness, 'Just call it the unwanted big brother syndrome.'

'Carley wants desperately to be independent,' Maggie said. 'All her life she's been protected by someone. She probably would have rejected anyone who tried to change her. She doesn't even want my help. You know, Carley's very proud.'

'Ah, the old Hale pride. It goeth before a fall, you know.' He threw her a quick, meaningful glance. 'I found that out the hard way.'

Maggie was just about to ask Jason what he meant when it happened. Perhaps the accident would not have been so bad had Jason not been talking about Carley and focusing so intently on her problems that his reflexes were just that much slower than usual. Or perhaps it was that glance in her direction that caused Jason to react a split-second too late, although, when they talked about it later, it was difficult even to make that assessment. Everything happened so quickly that Maggie caught only a flash of brown and white, an instant impression of antlers. The deer streaked across the car's path and Jason, to avoid hitting him, slammed hard on the brakes. The deer made it safely across the road, but the car skidded madly as its tyres tried to grip the road. The back end swung out, turning them in a rapid circle, and the car was then flung, by its own momentum, on to the side of the road and down an embankment where it crashed into the bole of a large tree. Maggie was thrown, with a violent jolt that knocked her breath right out of her, against the strap of her seat belt. Her head swung forward and then back again. Glass shattered, metal crumpled into accordion shapes, there was a great ripping sound as a door broke off, and her own scream echoed horribly in her ears.

Although the accident itself only took seconds, to Maggie it seemed as if it had gone on forever. She never lost consciousness, but she lost all sense of time and place. When it was over and there was no more motion, she still felt the violence in her head and her eyes couldn't seem to focus. For a few minutes, she simply sat there, tilted slightly at an angle, trying desperately hard to get her breath back and to understand where she was and what had happened. Slowly, her vision cleared and she blinked at the reflection of the sun off the hood of the car as it angled straight into her eyes. Then the sounds came to her. Because the car was leaning sideways, one wheel was free and spinning, making a humming sound. The clock on the dashboard had, miraculously, remained unscathed. It ticked loudly, its hands precisely set at 5:32. Overhead, a lone sparrow chirped from its perch in a low-hanging branch.

Maggie took a deep breath and felt the burning sensation in her chest subside. Her neck ached slightly and there was a new pain in the back of her left hand which came from a bruise that was starting to swell and throb. She rubbed it and then focused on the knee of the man next to her. Suddenly, it all came back to her; the deer, the sickening skid, the shock as the back end of the car crashed into the tree.

'Oh, God,' she whispered as she turned to look at Jason.

He was frighteningly still. His seat belt had also kept him in place, but the door on his side was gone, and it was obvious that he'd been thrown sideways, his head smashing into the ripped metal of the jamb. His eyes were closed and, although she could hear him breathing, Maggie discerned no other motion but the slight rise and fall of his chest.

Tentatively, she touched his shoulder but there was no response. 'Jason?' Maggie said and then louder, 'Jason!'

There was nothing but that shallow breathing, and Maggie felt fear knot her stomach. She fumbled with her seatbelt, unstrapped it and then leaned over him. His face was grey beneath the tan, the shadow of his dark beard prominent against the skin. Blood, bright red and glistening in the sunlight, dripped steadily from a gash in his forehead on to the shoulder of his shirt, turning its blue to a dark, damp purple. Her knowledge of first aid was only rudimentary, and she knew that her ability to move Jason, if that was wise in the first place, was limited. Maggie helplessly took one of Jason's hands and, rubbing it feverishly between hers, called him by his name, over and over again, her eyes filling with tears.

It was a desperate litany. 'Jason, Jason, wake up, Jason, open your eyes, Jason. . . .' But it had no effect, and Maggie felt the hysteria rising within her, a frantic sensation that filled her chest like a great balloon and threatened to explode out of her. She had always thought that she was the type who would be cool and calm when catastrophe struck, but she was nothing of the kind. Every shred of composure seemed to have deserted her as she clung to Jason's lifeless hand and begged him to come to consciousness. And it seemed impossible to her that squirrels could chatter in the underbrush or the sun could still be shining through the leaves of overhead trees. There was something horrible and hateful about a world that could go on about its business, oblivious to Jason's frightening lack of response and her own misery.

Suddenly, there was the screech of tyres from above the embankment as a pick-up truck came to a halt and an anxious voice called, 'Is everyone okay down there?'

Relief flowed into her like a flood. 'No,' she called out, 'there's a man hurt and unconscious!'

The two men in the pick-up proved to be helpful and efficient. One of them sped back into Fayetteville to alert the police and hospital; the other stayed with Maggie, helped her get out of the car and, ripping off his shirt, tried to use pieces of it to staunch the flow of blood from Jason's head. Although he kept reassuring her that Jason wasn't as bad as he looked, Maggie prowled around the car on legs that were barely steady and wrung her hands so hard that the next day they ached from the way she had clenched them together.

'You're darn lucky, you know,' the man said as they waited for the ambulance, 'that you hit that tree from behind. If it had been the front of the car, you might have been trapped in there.'

But Maggie gave him an uncertain smile, thinking what cold comfort it was to realise how much worse it might have been. She rubbed her injured hand and walked around the car, leaning down to pick up her hat which had been flung near to a tree. Her hands trembled as she turned its brim around in her fingers. Its white straw was clean and undented; it didn't look as if it had been in an accident in which a car had been a write-off and a man hurt to the point of unconsciousness. The hat, as fresh and as perky as a newly opened daisy, brought her back to another time, seemingly years ago, when she and Jason were driving down the highway, their voices low and intimate and friendly.

The Fayetteville Hospital had fifteen beds, two doctors and three nurses. They were all very kind and very reassuring. Jason was whisked into a separate room while Maggie was given a thorough going over by one physician who pronounced her healthy but in a slight state of shock. She was trembling so badly now that the worst was over and her adrenalin had stopped flowing, that her teeth clattered together, the noise audible in the small examining room. They injected her with a sedative, promised to phone Dragon's Point and told her that Jason would be fine. He had finally came around and was diagnosed as having a mild concussion and a cut that required stitching. Both of them were to stay overnight in the hospital for observation.

The sedative knocked Maggie out entirely, and she slept like a baby, hardly moving, her body and mind healing during the long hours of the night. When she woke the next morning to the cheerful administrations of a nurse who was pulling aside the curtain that had surrounded her bed, Maggie sat straight up and said groggily, 'Jason?'

'Your husband's doing just fine, Mrs Hale.' Maggie opened her mouth to object and say that she wasn't married to Jason, when the nurse went on, 'He's up, eating his breakfast and giving us a hard time. A handsome devil.'

She was an older woman, plump, grey-haired and motherly, and, if that was her reaction to Jason's obvious charms, Maggie sourly wondered how the other nurses, the younger ones, were doing. She found out about half-an-hour later when, finally presentable in a bathrobe and hospital gown, she wandered down to Jason's room and discovered that he was surrounded by women; two nurses, an aide and the hospital's receptionist. He was sitting up in bed, his head swathed in a bandage that made him look like a pirate, and he must have just cracked a joke because the women were all laughing. Someone must have shaved and washed him that morning because he looked remarkably good for a man with concussion and an injury.

'Maggie,' he said when he caught sight of her and the

bevy of adoring females evaporated, leaving the room empty except for the two of them. 'How are you?'

She perched on the edge of the bed. 'I'm fine,' she said. 'You were the one that was hurt.'

'They say I'm going to survive. Hey, is the back of your hospital gown as open as mine?' He reached out to test it and Maggie pulled back.

'Shame on you,' she said, although her heart lifted at the strength in his voice and the teasing tone. The Jason she had known was back. 'This is a public institution.'

'A man's interest in sex is directly related to the state of his health.'

'If you think, I'm going to let you test your health on me, then you have a few. . . .'

'Mrs Hale,' the doctor said as he came in, 'what do you think of our patient?' He was a small man with a moustache and horn-rimmed glasses, wearing a white coat with a stethoscope around his neck.

'I'm afraid . . .' Maggie began, but Jason interrupted, a conspiratorial light in his eyes.

'My wife doesn't like me in bandages,' he said. 'And she's worried that the stitches will ruin my looks.'

'Oh, don't worry, Mrs Hale, I was very careful and the cut was above the hairline. Once it's healed and the ahir grows back, he should be just as handsome as ever.'

'He's not. . . .'

'And as for this bandage,' the doctor probed gently at Jason's head, 'it won't be on for long.'

Maggie gave up and ignored Jason's grin. 'What about the concussion?'

'Not bad. His eyes look fine, there's steady balance, no nausea. We've got great hopes for this one.' The doctor patted Jason's shoulder. 'You can be discharged this afternoon, but I'll want to have a look at those stitches in a few days.'

When the doctor left the room, he shut the door behind him, a considerate motion for a married couple and one that made Jason say with a laugh, 'So much for public institutions. I do believe the fine doctor wants to give us a little bit of privacy.' He grabbed her hand. 'Let's make the most of it.'

'Jason . . .' Maggie warned, but he was too strong for her. Before she knew it she was lying beside him and he had his arm wrapped around her waist. 'This . . . this bed is too narrow.'

'The better to get close to you.' He nuzzled her neck. 'You've been hurt.'

'Mmmm—the better to heal me. Kiss me, Maggie, I know it will make my head feel better.'

'Does it hurt now?' she asked in alarm.

'No, but it will if you don't kiss me.'

'Jason, you're incorrigible.'

'I know, darling, that's half the fun.'

The kiss was long and sweet and wonderful, and Maggie melted beneath it, not realising until the moment Jason's lips touched hers how much she had been starved for the contact with him. She had not known that she wanted him to kiss her; she had not known that she longed for the feel of him against her. Her free hand slid over his shoulder, down to his back where the hospital gown was held together by bows. She slid her hand beneath them and touched the sleek muscularity of his back. Jason murmured his appreciation, and his tongue slid against hers, seeking a closer intimacy, and his hand rose to cup the fullness of her breast, his warmth solid and satisfying. Maggie may have been afraid of sex in the abstract, but in the flesh her fear simply evaporated as if it had never existed. There was something healing about this kiss. They had both been brushed by the chill of death, and this physical meeting was a reaffirmation of life, the attraction that blazed between them vital and enriching.

'Oh, Maggie,' Jason said with a sigh, 'we should do this more often.'

'You'd get spoiled,' she said, smiling as she bent her head in the crook of his arm.

'I need spoiling.'

'Hah!'

'Seriously. I'm a sad case, I don't get enough tender, loving care.'

'Poor baby.'

'You're laughing at me,' he said reproachfully, 'a man in a hospital bed with stitches in his head.'

'Waited on hand and foot by willing nurses.'

'Ah—do I hear just the tiniest note of jealousy?'

Maggie could tell that Jason was smiling and she gave him a slight jab to the solar plexus. 'Certainly not.'

'Ouch. I'd let *you* give me a bed bath anytime.'

'I bet you say that to all the girls—seductive line number 154, along with "Can I show you my etchings?" and "Haven't I seen you some place before?"'

Jason groaned. 'You sure know how to cut down a guy's ego.'

Maggie couldn't help it; the words seem to come forth of their own accord. 'That's ... what Nicholas said.'

Jason shifted a bit so that he could lean on his elbow and look down into Maggie's face. 'What did he say?'

Maggie glanced up at him and only saw concern in those golden eyes. 'He said I was too aggressive ... not feminine enough.'

'Why?'

Maggie gave a small, unhappy shrug. 'I don't know.'

'Because you acted like yourself?'

'Yes,' she said slowly, 'I suppose I acted like myself.'

'And he was threatened by it?'

'Maybe he was right.'

Jason gave her a little shake. 'Where's the Maggie Jordan confidence?'

'I'm not like other women,' she said defiantly.

'No,' said Jason.

'I'm not feminine in the traditional sense. I don't kowtow to men's egos and I like to speak my mind.'

'I've noticed.'

'I'm not . . . soft.'

'Is that bad?'

'Nicholas thought so.'

'Nicholas,' Jason said in clipped tones, 'is a fatuous ass.'

Maggie smiled then. 'He wouldn't have liked that epithet.'

'He would have deserved it.'

'It's very nice of you, Mr Hale, to come to my defence.'

Jason pulled her around so that they were facing each other once again. 'Maggie, we haven't known each other all that long—two and a half weeks?—but I think that I. . . .' He paused and then started again as if the words he were about to say were awkward and difficult. 'I've never thought that I would meet a woman who suited. . . .' He paused and cursed. 'Hell, I'm not managing this very well, am I?'

Maggie may have been hard and tough, but something within her went very feminine at Jason's words, something that was soft and warm and utterly delighted at his obvious confusion. She didn't know precisely what he was going to say, but the gist of it came across to her very clearly. It made the hospital room with its cold steel and white decor disappear so that the two of them seemed to be enclosed in a space that was uniquely their own, a moment in time when nothing mattered but their eyes meeting, the warmth of Jason's arm around her, the rueful look of his mouth at his own inability to say what he wanted, her ready anticipation.

'I haven't felt this adolescent,' Jason said, 'since I was fourteen.'

'Really.'

He grinned down at her. 'You're not going to help, are you?'

Maggie shook her head. 'I like it when you stammer; it gives you an appealing, boyish air.'

Jason laughed then and pulled her up to him, burying his face in her hair. 'Maggie,' he began, 'I. . . .'

There was a knock at the door; small, discreet but loud enough to startle and make them spring apart. By the time the door was opened, Maggie was sitting in a chair beside the hospital bed, smoothing her hair, and Jason was leaning back against the pillows, the covers tucked under his arms. Theodore entered carrying a small suitcase with Carley behind him, her face partially hidden behind an enormous bouquet of yellow mums.

'Surprise!' she cried gaily, and Maggie saw Jason give her flushed face an appraising look. 'Flowers, chocolates, extra clothes and a loving note from your insurance agent.'

Theodore shook his head. 'I always said you were a crazy driver.'

'A deer ran in front of us,' Maggie objected. 'It wasn't Jason's fault.'

Theodore clucked like a scolding mother hen. 'And look at that bandage. Ten stitches, the doctor told me, and. . . .'

The talk was bright, cheerful, hospital-type conversation. Carley put the flowers on a table beside Jason's bed, bringing a touch of sunshine into the room, and popped open the box of chocolates, passing them around and insisting that everyone take a candy. Theodore sat in the other chair and asked precise medical questions about Jason's condition. Maggie joined in for a while and then sat back, letting the voices fade. She watched Jason's face as he talked, noticed the pallor beneath his skin and guessed that his stitches were hurting him more than he let on. He smiled and ran his hand over his hair above the line of the bandage; he laughed once and threw his head back, the muscular column of his throat exposed to her view.

Maggie clenched her hands in her lap and suddenly understood it all. She had never been so attracted to a man before; not even Nicholas had inspired in her a desire so strong that she had longed to be with him. Yet, Jason brought out that need in her, and it was one that she wasn't accustomed to. Maggie was used to being independent but she had discovered that she wanted to be with Jason—all the time. And the attraction wasn't only physical; there was a meeting of minds between them that took her breath away. Their intellects matched like interlocking pieces of a jigsaw puzzle.

Jason knew it; he had realised it long before Maggie had ever acknowledged the existence of the two of them as a couple. She couldn't know what Jason would have told her had Carley and Theodore not arrived, but she suspected that he had wanted to express this feeling to her and, because it had never happened to him before, he had been awkward and inarticulate. Maggie could understand that; she had never been in love before and she wouldn't have known how to put it into words. All her cleverness deserted her at the thought of discussing the emotion that had grown so secretly in her heart.

Did Jason love her in return? Maggie remembered that soft golden glow in his eyes as he looked down at her and suspected that he did. It filled her with a joy that nothing could diminish; not even the thought of Oliver's suspicions. Maggie discovered that she didn't believe in them, not one little bit, and she was now firmly convinced that the RCMP investigations would prove her out. Jason couldn't be dealing in drugs; everything about him pointed in the opposite direction. How could a man who loved animals, family and nature be involved with a drug that destroyed people? It didn't make sense; it was absolutely and patently the most ridiculous thing she'd ever heard of.

Jason was saying something about Maggie and he reached over and took her hand, his smile warm and intimate, and she smiled right back. She had fallen headlong in love with him; she knew that now, and the force of loving him swept everything else aside. And, because she was the type of person who is accustomed to making independent and often contrary decisions without fear or concern, Maggie felt a supreme confidence in her choice. To hell with Oliver and his crazy ideas, she thought with a soaring triumph. To hell with him.

# CHAPTER SEVEN

DAMN stitches. They itched and pulled at his skin and bothered him when he tried to sleep at night. Jason found himself moving restlessly in bed, twisting the sheets around to the point that he found himself in a horrible tangle and ultimately staring up at the ceiling, awaiting that elusive state of sleep. He hated taking pills, even aspirin, so he suffered the consequences. Stoicism, he thought ruefully as he turned over for the umpteenth time and released his legs from the binds of the blanket, had its bad moments, but his misery hadn't entirely gone to waste. The enforced inactivity and irritating insomnia had their benefits. He had got more thinking done since the car accident than he had for months, and there was something about that brush with death, that sudden realisation of the fragility of life, that had given Jason food for thought. He had, slowly and thoroughly, dissected the past, mulled over the present and speculated about the future.

Business, he had decided, looked good although the expansion was a bit risky and would require new markets and hiring new men. Still, Jason liked a challenge and expanding into someone else's territory was the kind of entrepreneurial challenge that he especially enjoyed. Theodore was against it, but Jason had slowly lost his trust in the older man. Not that it was Theodore's fault exactly; Emma's illness and death had changed him. His keenness had been dulled and the shrewd way he had viewed the business world had disappeared as worries and grief overwhelmed him. Jason still left Theodore in charge of the home office, that required only a minimum of supervision since things were running smoothly, but he no longer took his advice on anything more serious than a minor personnel problem. And he was far too soft-hearted to retire the older man. Theodore had stuck with him through the good times and the bad; Jason had decided months ago that he'd let Theodore determine when retirement was ripe. There was enough fat in the company to keep on an old, and once highly valued, employee.

Of course, there was more to life than Hale Enterprises, and that's where the complications began. Take Carley, for example. He had watched her turn from a lovely, carefree and joyous girl to a woman with shadows in her eyes and a lifestyle that was dangerous. He hadn't really been surprised to learn that she was on drugs—it was the logical outcome of too much partying with the wrong kind of people, of days spent in bed and nights spent in bars, of a past that held an adulterous husband, a lost baby and a streak of insecurity that ran a mile wide. Jason had always believed that Carley's choice of husband had been crucial, and Alex had been a disaster. She had needed someone with a sense of responsibility, a desire to be paternalistic and an appreciation of her own particular brand of woman and child. Alex had had none of the proper qualifications, and Jason had been appalled when Carley had announced her engagement. He hadn't known Alex as anything but a casual acquaintance, but the other man's reputation was well known to those who moved in Toronto's financial circles. He was suave, smooth and an operator with women. Jason had always believed that Alex was after Carley's money.

He turned over again in bed and thought how useless it was to cry over spilled milk. Rehashing the past in Carley's case was useless; it was necessary to pick up the pieces now, to find the right doctor for her, to get her off drugs and away from the exploitation of people like David Moss. Jason wasn't sure how he was going to do it, but he also knew that he'd keep on trying no matter how resistant she was. He had been honest when he'd told Maggie how he felt about Carley. She'd been the sister he never had, the child he'd never conceived, a blonde and feminine delight in his parent's house. He'd been hooked on her from the moment he had seen her as a boy of thirteen, gingerly taking a pink bundle out of his aunt's arms and staring down at round cheeks shaded by incredibly long lashes and a mouth that made tiny sucking motions.

The first seed of fatherhood had been sown then, Jason thought wryly, a seed that had lain dormant for years only to blossom forth now when he had reached the ripe old age of thirty-seven. He liked babies, he liked children. He wanted to have a son with strong limbs and a daughter with curls he could twist around his finger. He knew how sexist that would sound to a feminist, but he couldn't help it. As he approached forty, Jason had discovered a strong streak of sentimentality and traditionalism in himself that he would have despised ten years earlier. As it was, he barely knew how to handle it now. It had altered the way that he thought about women and relationships; it had made him crave stability and security; and it was the power driving him towards Maggie Jordan with a stunning recklessness. All the protective devices that he'd cultivated in twenty years of maintaining his status as a bachelor seemed to be evaporating into thin air.

It had come as quite a shock to discover himself on the verge of telling Maggie that he loved her. He hadn't even known he was going to say it until the words had trembled on his lips, waiting to pour forth into the silence. And the truth was that he hadn't even known that he felt that way until he had found himself drowning in those blue eyes, sinking into the depths of them and discovering that he never wanted to surface. Jason had started his approach to Maggie with the thought of an affair in his mind. He had been candid, telling her how well they suited one another. It was true that he'd stammered a bit and that there was something about the amusement in Maggie's eyes that had made him feel like a schoolboy, but he had enjoyed the sensation. Although they had both been carrying on a flirtation for the past three weeks, Maggie was the type of woman who demanded honesty and, when the time came, Jason had known that she would see through a façade of sophistication and mock any attempt he made to coat his proposal with glib, smooth words.

So he'd intended to be frank, to suggest that they consider embarking on a serious and monogamous affair. He knew that Maggie was bored with her job in Ottawa, and he knew of half-a-dozen companies in Toronto that would hire her on his say so. Hell, she could even work for him if she wished. He had envisioned separate apartments at first, thinking that they'd go at it slowly, learn to know one another better and have time to consider the options. If they found that they were as compatible sexually as they were mentally, then they could live together or decide to get married. Jason had thought this was a rational, logical approach and one that someone as wary as Maggie might prefer. He'd also known that it sounded cold and calculated, but he'd tried just about everything else with Maggie, and nothing had succeeded. He'd been charming, seductive, sexy, accommodating, perceptive, and sympathetic. There was nothing left but asking her outright if she'd be willing to sleep with him.

So he had started only to discover that his proposal, this simple and straightforward request, was somehow getting tangled and lost in something else. Feelings had surged up in him that had nothing to do with sex and a lot to do with that unhappy and lost look in Maggie's eyes when she'd talked about Nicholas. He had discovered how violently he hated this apparition from Maggie's past, this man whose name cropped up when they were embracing and whose memory had the power to make her eyes darken in sadness. Jealousy of this lover had made him tighten his arms around her and a need to protect her had made him pull her closer. These emotions, at first separate and distinct, had gathered to make a whole, filling him with an indescribable sensation, a caring and tenderness that had slowly taken shape as letters, as words, as the sentence, 'I love you'. Jason had never said it to any other woman, had never even thought he would feel the power of love, but when he had held Maggie in his arms, her softness against him, the words had seemingly come out of nowhere, and he had known that they were true.

He turned over once again, shook the sheets to straighten them and then tucked his arms behind his head. Imagine falling in love in two and one-half weeks after years of resisting any suggestion that love was possible, and imagine falling in love with a woman like Maggie. She wasn't the type who would make his life easy; Jason knew that. She was going to be hell on wheels. He grinned up at the darkened ceiling as he thought about marriage to Maggie. There were all the potential conflicts of any live-in relationship; who would make the meals, take out the garbage, keep the chequebook. He suspected that every item would be up for an intense negotiation, and that bargaining with Maggie was going to be extraordinary. Another man might have been daunted at the idea of co-habitating with a woman who considered herself anyone's equal, but Jason rather relished the idea. Maggie rarely said anything that wasn't provoking, interesting, maddening or exhilarating; she would keep him perpetually teetering on his toes.

And then, of course, there was that overwhelming sexual attraction. It was like the icing on the cake, a glorious and unexpected gift that life, in its careless fashion, had bestowed upon him. Jason knew how precious that passion was; it mustn't be squandered, wasted or abused. When the moment came that he and

Maggie finally made love, it would have to take place in the right circumstances and at the right time. He didn't want to hurry the pace of their relationship or push Maggie beyond her limits. He now had a good idea of what had transpired in her affair with Nicholas, and he was convinced that Maggie's deepest feelings about her mother were the driving force behind her resistance to his overtures. Jason didn't want to force her; he didn't want Maggie to go to bed with him against her will. He wanted her to come to him with a desire as great as his own; in love, in wanting and in tenderness.

Yes, Jason thought, as he turned over on to his side and closed his eyes, finally feeling a warm and welcome drowsiness return, he'd wait for Maggie. She would let him know when the time was right. He had seen the softness in her eyes, that first sign of yielding, and he knew with all the confidence of a man who has had many women that it was merely a beginning to a deeper commitment, the ultimate union. The thought of that coming together, the final culmination of eyes meeting, of flirtatious conversation, of kisses caught in the heat of the sun, made him smile into the darkness. Yes, Maggie was well worth waiting for; the first and only woman he had ever met who was.

'Oliver?'

'Maggie, you were supposed to phone me yesterday!'

'I'm sorry,' Maggie said contritely, 'but I couldn't Jason had a car accident and I was with him.'

Oliver's voice was sharp. 'What kind of an accident?'

'A deer ran across the road and we skidded trying to avoid it.'

Was there a hint of relief in Oliver's voice? 'Are you okay?'

'I'm fine. Jason had a mild concussion and a cut on his forehead. The car was a write-off.'

'Is Hale in bad shape?'

'He's in a bit of pain, I think. He's spending most of his time in bed.'

'Anything else of interest up there?'

Maggie found herself twisting the telephone cord around her finger as tightly as it would go. She was at the pay phone in Merrick, and the small closed-in booth was swelteringly hot. Beads of perspiration were forming on her upper lip and the receiver was slippery in her hand.

'Oliver, if I tell you this, you must promise me that you won't do anything to hurt Carley.' Maggie swallowed and then went on, convinced that what she was about to do was the best thing considering the circumstances. 'I don't want her to have to . . . go to jail or be put under arrest.'

Oliver sounded bewildered. 'Carley?'

'Oh, she's not involved in the heroin business, but I found drugs in her room, barbituates, uppers and downers.'

'I see.'

'David Moss is her supplier.'

'Hmmm.'

Oliver's noncommittal murmur made Maggie apprehensive. 'You wouldn't do anything to Carley, would you?' she said quickly. 'Isn't David the one who you should. . . .'

'Maggie, calm down. We're not interested in hurting victims; we want to get the people who are abusing them. You don't have to worry about us going after your friend. All we might want from her is information on the people she's dealing with.'

'When would you . . .?'

'Not for a while,' Oliver said soothingly, 'and in the gentlest way possible. Now, is there anything else of interest up there?'

Maggie hesitated and then plunged in. 'I don't think Jason is your heroin supplier.'

'Oh?'

'He can't be; he's a ... decent man, Oliver. He really is.' Oliver's silence at the other end should have warned Maggie but she kept on going. 'He's gentle, kind, caring and honest. He would no sooner have dealings in drugs than. . . .'

'Have you brought the subject up with him?'

'Of course not, but I can tell what he's like.' Maggie sought desperately for evidence to convince an obviously reluctant Oliver of her belief in Jason. 'He was horrified to hear about Carley.'

'She's his niece.'

'But the whole idea of the drugs upset him!'

'Maggie, there are many criminals who care as much about their families as the next person. In some cases, they live seemingly ordinary lives; they participate in their communities, support local churches, go to PTA meetings. They love their wives, their children and their dogs, but that doesn't stop them from committing crimes. In fact, some of the upper echelon drug types who don't actually do the pushing or the thug work appear to be solid, respectable citizens.'

'I don't believe Jason is one of those,' Maggie said firmly.

Oliver's voice was cool. 'It sounds to me as if you're letting personal feelings interfere with your reporting.'

'It's easy for you to seem so objective from your armchair in Ottwa, Oliver, but you'd think differently if you were up here with me. You'd see what a wonderful person he is.'

'Maggie,' Oliver said with incredulity, 'it sounds as if you've fallen in love with him!'

'I. . . .' She hesitated.

Oliver's implacability came right through the receiver. 'The truth, Maggie.'

'I ... think I have.'

There was a long silence, and Maggie could just imagine Oliver's reaction. She could even see him sitting at his desk at RCMP headquarters, the phone to his ear, his body slumped against the seat, one hand absentmindedly rubbing the spot on his nose where his glasses usually sat, an attitude comprised of shock and dismay.

'I don't believe this,' he finally said.

'I'm sorry,' Maggie said helplessly, leaning against the hot wall of the booth and then flinching when the metal came in contact with her bare shoulder. Outside, a large truck rumbled down the highway, making the booth shake and causing huge swirls of brown dust to fill the air.

'You haven't said anything to Hale about these phone calls, have you?'

'No, Oliver, of course not.'

'When are you leaving Dragon's Point?'

'In about four days.'

'Now, listen carefully. I want you to phone me on Thursday, two days from now, from the phone booth in Merrick at nine o'clock in the morning.'

'Why?'

'I'm going to be out all day and that's the only time I can be reached.'

'But. . . .'

'Maggie, just do as I say, all right?'

Her voice was low and meek. 'Okay.'

Oliver sighed. 'And do me a favour, please. Don't give Jason any hint of what you've been doing until we get this thing solved.'

'I won't.'

'And Maggie, for god's sake, take care of yourself. Don't trust anyone, don't talk to anyone, you've only got to hold on for a few days now.'

'I promise, but, Oliver . . .?'

'Yes.'

'You'll keep an open mind about Jason, won't you?'

'For your sake,' he said.

Maggie could tell that Oliver was just saying that to

placate her. 'I just *know* he's not the man you're looking for.'

'We'll see.'

'Oliver, I have good instincts about people,' she began, her voice desperate, 'and I'm positive. . . .'

Oliver's voice was firm, cool and dismissive. 'Goodbye, Maggie. Remember, Thursday at nine from the phone booth.'

The telephone receiver clicked, and Maggie pulled it slowly away from her ear. The heat in the booth had gone from being uncomfortable to oppressive, and she felt faint, slightly nauseous and very tired. The air outside was cooler, but Maggie didn't leave the booth. Instead, she put the receiver on its hook and, leaning her forehead against the top of the telephone, closed her eyes, willing all thought away and concentrating as hard as she could on the sensation of that cool ridge pressed so tightly against her skin.

Jason still didn't look himself, but Maggie thought that his face had regained most of its colour, and he certainly looked less barbaric now that his stitches were covered by a small bandage rather than the enormous one that had been wrapped around his head at a rakish angle. He had emerged from his bedroom for breakfast, dressed in blue shorts and a white t-shirt, eaten a decent meal and spent the morning fishing from the dock. He hadn't caught anything, but Maggie rather suspected that he hadn't wanted to. He seemed more interested in sitting in the sun, letting the breeze lift his hair and listening to the gentle sounds of the lake as it slapped up against the dock's wooden pillars.

Theodore and Carley drove to Fayetteville to handle the disposition of Jason's wrecked car, and Maggie busied herself in the house. At noon, she made up a tray with ham sandwiches and coffee and brought it down to the dock, but Jason had fallen asleep and she didn't

have the heart to wake him. She put her hand down on
Hercules' head as he rose to greet her, thinking that it
would have been criminal to wake a man who so
obviously needed his sleep as Jason. His head was
leaning against the high back of the chair, a dark curve
of hair fell over his forehead and long lashes lay like
black crescents on his cheekbones. The fishing rod was
loose in his hands and his legs were spread out before
him; dark-haired, muscular and shapely for a man. She
stared at him for a time, noticing the strong line of his
jaw, the latent power of a shoulder beneath his t-shirt,
the leanness of his fingers. Maggie wondered what it
would be like to see him nude, to have him with her on
a bed, that body, hard and warm, pressing her down
against the mattress. The thought made her flush, and
she looked away, suddenly ashamed at her open and
worshipping voyeurism.

Jason slept on, and Maggie carefully lowered herself
to the dock beside the resting Hercules. She let the dog
have one-half of a ham sandwich, ate the other half and
threw the crusts into the water where a dozen minnows
immediately rose to the surface and began to rip and
tear at the bread. She then dangled her feet in the water,
frightening away most of the fish except for a couple of
brave souls that nibbled at her toes. A ray of sun cut
through the surface of the lake, lighting its depths to a
greenish-gold and Maggie, leaning back on her hands,
thought how peaceful it was to be sitting on the dock
beside the man that she loved, knowing that his sleep
was healing and that, despite her horrible phone call to
Oliver and all of his disclaimers to the contrary, Jason
was as innocent as the day was long.

She had decided that policemen were paid to be
suspicious; it was a part and parcel of their duties, an
attitude they assumed when they pulled on their
uniforms and clipped the badges to their pockets.
Whereas she believed that a man was innocent until
proven guilty, Oliver assumed the reverse: that he was

guilty until proven innocent. Well, it would all come to
the same thing in the end, she decided with the
confidence that comes from love. The outcome of the
RCMP investigations would demonstrate Jason's lack
of involvement in drugs. She had no idea who was
smuggling heroin in the Hale Enterprises shipments
from Singapore, and she didn't much care. As long as,
when the unveiling came, Jason would stand free and
innocent.

The future had a feeling to it that Maggie had never
experienced; a brightness, a clarity, a golden glow. For
years, she had seen nothing before her but taking care
of the house, looking after Daniel and going to work.
Nicholas had entered her life and briefly given it some
meaning, but when he was gone, that small illumination
had been blown out, like a candle flame obliterated in a
gust of cold wind. Maggie had lost all hope then of
leading the kind of life other women seemed to find
with such ease. Most men seemed to find her too
aggressive, too masculine for their taste, and underneath
she had never believed that she could successfully be a
wife or a mother. She had tried to recover the calm and
stoicism that had been her characteristics before
Nicholas' entry into her life, but their affair made that
impossible. During the height of it, the Pandora's box
of her emotions had opened and a host of longings had
flown out into the air, visible and clamorous.

She wanted a husband and children. She wanted to
prove that she wasn't her mother; that unlike Sandra,
she had enough love to hold a family together, to be
steadfast, to be caring. She wanted a daughter that she
could raise from infancy to adulthood, relishing each
stage, helping and guiding her to become a woman.
And she wanted a man in her life; a lover, a companion,
a friend, and a father all rolled into one. For all her
fierce independence, Maggie found within herself an
intense desire to need and be needed. It had been
frightening to have that core of loneliness revealed; it

made her feel vulnerable and open. She had tried to shut it away and ignore its incessant demands, and she had been successful until Jason had come into her life, forcing her desires, for sex, for a family and for love, out of their dark, hiding places and into the uncompromising light of day.

She hadn't thanked Jason for that; at first, she'd recoiled from his honesty, his perceptions and the emotions he had provoked, but lately she had realised that she trusted him and was no longer threatened by the way he could see into her heart and soul. Jason respected her; he appreciated the turn of her mind, the way she approached life, the toughness she had acquired in order to survive. He had let her know, by words and actions, that she was a special woman, unique and separate. When they'd first met, Maggie had sensed his boredom, that jaded amusement of life, but it was gone now. And in its place, she thought with a smile that could not be restrained, was love.

'They must be good,' Jason said.

Maggie glanced around. 'Good?'

'Your thoughts—you're smiling.'

'It's nice out here in the sun.'

'Why can't you admit to being happy?'

'Happy?'

He smiled down at her. 'Sure—it doesn't hurt.'

Happy—Jason was right; she *was* happy. Despite Oliver's suspicions, the fact that her vacation was almost over and her imminent return to Daniel and her job, Maggie was happy. Nothing in the future was certain, but its shape had changed. It shimmered just beyond view; elusive and indistinguishable yet rich with promise.

'All right,' she said, 'I'm happy. Are you?'

Jason leaned his head back again. 'Actually, I've been thinking about my mortality.'

'That sounds dangerous,' she said lightly.

'The car accident brought it on.'

'Ah—your typical brush-with-death syndrome.'

'I've been giving some serious thought to my past, present and future. Do you want to know what I've concluded?'

'What?'

'That I need a wife.'

There was more to this conversation than appeared on the surface, but Maggie was quite willing to follow Jason's lead in keeping it light, amusing and superficial. 'A wife?' she asked with astonishment. 'Capital A, capital W?'

'The real McCoy.'

'Female, under forty and in good health?'

Jason's eyes glinted in amusement. 'I'd have to check her dental records first, of course. I wouldn't want a woman with bad teeth.'

'And a strong heart and well-developed muscles,' Maggie agreed. 'She'd have to make your meals, iron your shirts, clean your house, bear your children and entertain your friends.'

'Actually,' he said softly. 'I was thinking of someone to love me.'

The words sent Maggie's heart into a small flutter, but she steadfastly contemplated her toes as they stuck up out of the water. 'Well,' she said, 'there's always the columns. Remember that ad we devised–"Eligible male", and all that.'

'I've decided against that. It seems to me that if I can't find a woman on my own to be my wife then I'm not very competent. Wouldn't you agree?'

'The personal touch should be more effective.'

There was a short silence between them then, and Hercules raised his white head to look from one to the other as if to say—get on with it. Jason finally spoke, his voice pensive as though he'd given the subject a lot of thought. 'Actually, I already have a cleaning service for my apartment, a caterer who does my dinners and a laundry down the street who does shirts. I think I could manage with a woman whose biceps were less developed.'

'Still,' Maggie said, 'marriage should be a fifty-fifty arrangement.'

'Like I take out the garbage, you buy the toothpaste?'

'Right.'

'You keep the car running and I cook the meals?'

'Yes.'

'You have the baby and I do the diapering?'

'Absolutely.'

'I make love to you and you make love to me?'

'Sex,' she said reprovingly, 'why does every conversation have to boil down to sex.'

Jason smiled. 'You make it sound like cabbage.'

'And you make it sound like the common denominator.'

'It's important, don't you think?'

'Absolutely essential—for procreation.'

Jason made a scolding sound. 'The puritan façade—just one of your many disguises.'

Maggie looked at him sideways. 'What disguises?'

'Secretive Maggie, flirtatious Maggie, prudish Maggie, sexy Maggie, innocent Maggie . . . shall I go on?'

'I'm *not* prudish.'

He grinned at her, his teeth white against his tan. 'Right—I made that one up. You do have your moments when your modesty completely deserts you.'

The memory of those moments made Maggie's cheeks pinken. 'I was suffering from sunstroke.'

'What a blow to my ego,' Jason said lightly. 'I'd got the distinct impression that my skilful lovemaking might have had something to do with it.'

'It might. . . .' She let her voice linger and Jason immediately picked it up.

'But . . .?'

Maggie gave him a smile. 'It didn't.'

Jason shook his head in mock-admiration. 'Did they mix nails in with your baby food?'

'Tacks, actually.'

A door slammed, and Carley emerged from the house and ran lightly down the steps to the dock. She was flushed from the heat but she gestured to them, making the V for victory sign with her fingers.

'Your car is in safe hands,' she said as she came up to Jason.

'Safe hands?'

'A real demolition expert. He has one of those machines that takes your car and makes it into a little package.' She demonstrated with her hands, making crushing motions. 'It's very neat and tidy.'

'And what about a new car?'

'If Theodore can get your bank to send the money up pronto, you'll soon be the proud owner of a red Maverick tomorrow. He's phoning right now.'

Jason asked, 'Red?'

'A screaming fire-engine red,' Carley confirmed, adding when Jason winced, 'Beggars can't be choosers.'

'True,' he said with a sigh. 'So sit down and give me the details. Does it have automatic transmission?'

Maggie sat back, swished her feet back and forth in the water and listened to the conversation. It struck her that Jason was taking a new tack with Carley. There were no more arguments, recriminations and accusations. As far as she knew, he'd not even brought up the subject of her use of drugs. When Maggie remembered Jason's words in the car, she realised that he had finally opted out of the role of Carley's substitute father. It was, she saw, a wise decision. Carley didn't respond to parental-style threats and anger. No matter how childish she might act at times, she needed to be handled with respect and concern. Even now as she and Jason talked lightly about cars, Maggie could see Carley visibly relaxing, and it occurred to her that Jason's influence would be far more powerful and effective if he acted as Carley's friend rather than her guardian. She thought that he must have come to that conclusion himself, because he was treating Carley with just the right amount of lighthearted banter and easygoing conversation. He was even making Carley laugh, a feat that required far more dexterity than it should.

Maggie smiled along with them, but the smile went far deeper. There was an inner part of her that was still laughing over the conversation she had just had with Jason. Nothing overt had been said; no arrangements made, but there had been a delicate negotiation just the same. The parameters of a relationship had been subtly hammered out along with the teasing, the flirtation and the seeming nonchalance. There had been a proposal hidden in the verbal camouflage; Jason's asking and her acceptance. She had seen a smiling acknowledgement of it in his eyes and knew it was reflected in her own. Maggie felt the glimmering future come closer, emerge into a hazy shape and beckon enticingly to her. A future that included love and commitment, sexual passion and children. Marriage to Jason Hale.

# CHAPTER EIGHT

THEODORE was acting strangely. Maggie first noticed it at breakfast the next morning when she happened to look up from buttering her toast and saw that Theodore's hands were shaking so badly he couldn't manage to spoon sugar into his coffee. She thought it odd and then dismissed it until later that morning when she came upon him sitting out on the porch staring over the lake. At first, she couldn't put her finger on what was wrong; then she saw what it was. Theodore, who was usually so neat, so tidy and precise, had not shaved that morning and his round jowls were bristling with fine grey stubs of hair. He looked slovenly and unkempt, and she had never before seen him looking anything but dapper and sharp. She spoke to him but he would only answer her in monosyllables, and he made it so obvious that he wanted to be left alone that Maggie had been forced to go, although she had felt uncomfortable at leaving him in such a state.

By that evening, everyone in the house was aware of Theodore's condition. Although he had rarely been a part of their activities, preferring, it had seemed, the solitude of his room or the company of a book, his strange behaviour had become very obvious. The trouble was that Theodore was drinking and, from the way it affected him, Maggie suspected that he wasn't a man who was accustomed to alcohol. At first, he had become voluble during dinner, his conversation both disjointed and, after a while, incomprehensible. Jason was the first to try to put the bottle of scotch away, but Theodore had gone after it and poured himself another generous portion. The three of them let Theodore ramble on throughout the meal but, after it was over, Jason had tried to convince him to sleep it off in his bedroom.

'I'm not tired,' Theodore said belligerently.

Jason was blunt. 'Theo, you're drunk.'

'I'm not.'

'You've managed to drink almost an entire bottle of scotch.'

'I'll buy you another.'

'I don't want you to buy me another one; I just want you to go and rest.'

'No.'

Although his voice wasn't slurred, it was hard for Theodore to walk in a straight line. It was excruciating to watch him rise from the table, fumble with his chair and try to maintain his balance. Maggie didn't think she'd ever seen anything so sad and pathetic as Theodore, still unshaven and dressed in a crumpled shirt and trousers, attempting to be dignified under the influence of too much alcohol. He got up from the table, weaved his way through the chairs in the living room and, miscalculating the doorway to the front porch, crashed into its sill. Jason and Carley were by his side in an instant, helping him up from the floor, picking up his glasses which he tried to put on with trembling fingers.

'Don't know where that came from,' he said.

It was obvious that the crash had unnerved him, because he now let Jason take his elbow. 'Theo, why don't you lie down?'

'Don't want to die,' mumbled Theodore.

'Die?' Carley exclaimed. 'Heavens, Theo, what are you talking about? You're perfectly safe here with us.'

Jason took Theodore's words in another light. 'You mustn't let Emma's death affect you this way.' He was leading the older man, very gently, towards his room. 'You're in perfect health.'

Theodore's brown eyes filled with tears, and he had a drunken man's lachrymose voice. 'Did it for Emma,' he said.

Jason was soothing. 'Of course, you did. You were wonderful to her.'

'The pain ... she cried ... did I tell you that?'

Maggie could hear Jason's calm tones as he helped Theodore down the corridor. 'It's over now,' he said. 'It's all over.'

Carley slumped down on the couch. 'I've never seen Theo like that,' she said sadly. 'He's falling apart.'

Maggie joined her. 'He must have been so close to his wife.'

Carley sighed. 'It was a love affair,' she said. 'They used to hold hands when they went for walks. I have little-girl memories of spending weekends with Uncle Theo and Aunt Emma. They weren't relatives, but they were so close to the family that for years I thought they were. I'd visit and be treated to all sorts of goodies. They always had candy in the house which Theo would hide for me so I'd have to search for it, and Emma always had the time to play cards with me. Their children were older than I was so I was treated like the baby in the family. The atmosphere in their house was very lovely and warm and sweet.'

'He's Jason's right-hand man, isn't he?'

'Was,' Carley said, 'I get the feeling that Jason can't give him the same sort of responsibilities any more. He wouldn't be able to handle them.'

Although she had been shocked by Theodore's drinking, Maggie was far more interested in Carley's problems, and she suddenly saw a chance to switch the conversation on to a more personal plane. She hadn't had a chance to talk to Carley since finding the drugs in her room, but she'd been looking for an opportunity ever since. 'Have you ever thought of working for Jason—seriously?'

Carley gave her a sideways glance. 'He's offered,' she said cautiously. 'You know that.'

'I think it would do you good.'

Carley's rebuttal was swift. 'I think it would have

been like working for my father. All guidance and precious little freedom. I told you before, Jason wants to run my life.'

Maggie saw a chance to help Jason's crusade. 'What do you think he would do if he knew you were on drugs?'

Carley tossed her blonde curls. 'Get on my case,' she said grimly. 'That's his favourite spot.'

'He knows,' Maggie said bluntly. 'I told him.'

Carley's mouth dropped open slightly. 'He does?' she finally asked.

'Yes.'

'Since when?'

'Since before the accident.'

'I . . . I don't believe it.'

'It's true.'

'But he hasn't said a word to me!'

Maggie gave a shrug. 'Maybe Jason doesn't really want to hassle you any more; maybe he's figured out that it just gets your back up.'

Carley looked down at her fingers where the nails had been bitten back to the quick. 'I wouldn't have thought he was so sensitive,' she muttered.

'He is—very sensitive.'

For a moment, Carley thought about that and then, suddenly, a smile played around her lips. 'Now, that's an about-face,' she said. 'A couple of weeks ago, you thought he was the world's biggest playboy.'

It was Maggie's turn to investigate her fingernails. Hers were long, shapely and gleaming with clear polish. 'I've changed my mind.'

The small smile turned into a grin. 'Oh, Maggie, I knew you'd fall for him. Who could resist those looks he's been giving you? Smouldering, passionate, sexy. I told you he was irresistible.'

Maggie tried to get her off the scent. 'I hate I-told-you-so's,' she said in a grumpy tone.

But Carley's glee couldn't be deterred. 'I'm trying to

imagine it,' she said. 'Jason Hale and Maggie Jordan. Maggie Hale. No, women are keeping their last names now. Maggie Jordan-Hale. Now, that has a ring to it.'

'Carley, we haven't even talked about marriage! Our acquaintance is only three weeks old.'

'I may be a cynic about my own life, Maggie, but I'm a romantic about others. I'd swear you were made for each other, and Jason's ripe for commitment. He's bored with most women; I've seen him politely turn off after two minutes of conversation.'

'I suppose I should be flattered then,' Maggie said dryly, 'that he was willing to give me the time of day.'

Carley shook her head with conviction. 'He's lucky to get you, too. I've watched you together; you keep him interested, he can never tell what you're thinking. You're a mysterious sort of person, Maggie.'

'Mysterious? Me?'

Carley appraised her. 'Mmmm—hidden thoughts behind those blue eyes.'

'That's ridiculous.'

Carley leaned earnestly forward. 'Jason needs stability and permanence. He's been rattling around for years, dating this woman and then that one. He wants a home, a wife and a family. You must realise that.'

'I do,' Maggie said softly, and then blushed at what she had revealed. She cleared her throat and added, 'He's said so.'

'And . . .?'

'Well, let's just say, I'm entertaining the possibilities.'

Carley leaned her head back and smiled up at the ceiling. 'Welcome to the family,' she said.

'Careful,' Maggie said with a little laugh, 'don't rush things yet.'

'Oh, I'm not rushing anything,' Carley said with a contented sigh. 'I'm just thinking how wonderful it will be when Jason can direct all that misguided fatherly zeal on to the unsuspecting heads of his own children.'

That night, after Maggie had got ready for bed and was sitting up against the pillows, dressed in a nightgown and reading a book, there was a knock on the door. She had, of course, known that this was coming. She had taken a long, hot bath, soaking under a foot of scented bubbles; she had given her hair its one hundred brush strokes so that it hung to her shoulders in gleaming chestnut waves; she had put on a new, crisply washed nightgown, her favourite one, a soft white cotton with blue ribbons that matched the colour of her eyes threaded through eyelets at the neck and on the sleeves. She had even got into bed and then, as an afterthought and with ironic mutterings about the practicality of the modern woman, she had gone to the bathroom one more time and, just in case, had used the form of birth control that she'd been fitted for during her affair with Nicholas.

Finally, she had arranged herself on the bed in a pose that was seemingly relaxed with the book resting on her chest, her legs crossed at the ankles. Only the lamp by her bed was lit so that the illumination in the room was gentle, the golden glow touching on her hair, a cheekbone, her shoulder, softening every angle or line and giving the room a romantic haze as if a filmy gauze covered every surface.

'Who is it?' she said, although she knew very well who it was.

'Jason—can I come in?'

'Yes.'

He was wearing jeans and a blue-checked shirt. His feet were bare and tracked damp marks on the carpet. His hair was wet and curling around his forehead, and Maggie realised that he had just had a shower. She couldn't restrain a small smile when she saw that he had also shaved: the complete male lover; clean, washed and with smooth chin.

'Why are you smiling?' Jason asked, sitting down in the chair opposite the bed.

'I'm thinking how odd this is—entertaining you in my room after hours.'

'This isn't a dorm.'

'No, but it sort of has that feeling to it, don't you think?'

'When I was in college,' he said, 'we had to sneak into the girls' rooms. I went to an American university that believed itself to be the guardian of our morals. This was before the era of co-ed living arrangements, and the girls' dorms had proctors, chaperoned hours for meeting and a rule that said the door had to be opened half-an-inch and three feet had to be on the floor.'

'Three feet?'

'Believe me,' Jason said, 'it was damn hard to achieve anything subversive with only one foot out of four on the horizontal. So I used to sneak in after curfew.'

'You didn't get caught?'

Jason put his hands behind his head and stretched, making the broad expanse of his chest arch upwards and causing Maggie to feel a soft sensation of heat start deep within her. 'Once,' he said reminiscently, 'a girl and I were in the throes of ... well, I'll leave that to your imagination ... and there was a quick knock on the door, a whisper that a proctor was doing a bed-check, and I was half-dressed and out of the window in under thirty seconds.' He gave a laugh. 'If I remember correctly, I almost lost my manhood on a drainpipe.'

'That would have been a loss to society,' Maggie said dryly.

Jason shook his head as if she'd delivered him a low blow. 'Why is it I have the feeling that the crown jewels aren't getting the respect they deserve?'

'Oh?' she said lightly. 'What do they deserve?'

Jason looked solemn as if they were discussing the weather, the latest rise in the bank rate, statistics on unemployment. 'Care,' he said, 'admiration, sympathy, appreciation, understanding.'

'They must be very . . .' Maggie sought for the right word, 'competent.'

'Highly,' he said, the green-and-gold eyes glinting at her. 'They've been approved.'

'Really? By whom?'

'There are standards in the industry, Miss Jordan. You must realise that.'

It was a very enjoyable conversation. They both knew why he had come, and Maggie had felt a flutter in her stomach all evening, an excitement that mixed both anticipation and apprehension. What had begun as a frisson of interest in the company of an attractive man had developed into an all-consuming and passionate desire to sleep with him. Despite her reservations about sex and her bad experiences with Nicholas, Maggie could hardly wait for Jason's lovemaking. For the past week, she had suffered every torment known to those whose physical desires are frustrated and unfulfilled. She had felt a thrill pass through her when he glanced at her, she'd gone weak if he touched her, she dreamt at night of erotic meetings, of touches on her skin, of limbs tangled together.

Maggie had been reduced to cold showers and long hikes; she had never known that the longing for a man's body could be so overwhelming. In comparison, her desire for Nicholas had been a pale facsimile of the real thing. And this longing had brought her to a deeper understanding of Sandra Jordan. She would never really know what her mother's motivation for leaving had been, but if sex had been part of it, then Maggie was now a sister in sympathy. Sexual desire, she had discovered, came out of nowhere as if conjured up by a magician's trick and then, finding a susceptible victim, grew until its strength was unsurpassed. In some ways, Maggie felt helpless against this power, dragged willy-nilly towards this night, towards the man who sat beside her bed, towards the moment when he would join her on it.

'How is Theodore?' she asked.

Jason only acknowledged her deliberate change of subject with a nod of his head. 'Sleeping it off.'

'I wonder what happened to make him drink like that?'

'It's been a slow disintegration,' Jason said sadly. 'This is just another step in the direction he's been going.'

The words came out of Maggie's mouth even before she realised the thought that had prompted them. 'Do you think it's dangerous to get so close to someone that you can't bear it when they're gone?'

'Do we have any choice?' Jason asked.

'What do you mean—choice?'

He gave a light shrug. 'It seems to me that trying to protect yourself from hurt also means that you can never have the kind of relationships that make life worth living. If Theo is suffering now, it's because he had thirty-five years of happiness. I don't doubt that, if he were given the choice, between those years with Emma and avoiding what he feels now, he'd choose Emma all over again. I've thought about it, you know, and I can't see that being isolated is worth it. Life is risky; to be happy, you have to take the risks.' He gave her a perceptive look. 'You're thinking about your mother, aren't you?'

Maggie gave him a smile that she meant to be natural but held a tremulous line. Of course, her words had been prompted by memories of Sandra; for most of her life, she had avoided the kind of commitment with other people that had the potential to be dangerous. She had learned, very early in life, that loving someone could prove to be extremely painful. 'A child doesn't have a choice about where it can invest its emotions,' she said slowly. 'A child can't help loving its parent, no matter how bad the parent is.'

Jason's voice was soft. 'What was she like?'

Maggie thought for a moment, her face pensive. 'I'm

not sure, you know. I was very young when she left. What I remember are flashes, images, odd moments caught in time. I don't have any memories of her with my father; I think they lived very separate lives, but I always seem to recall her things; her clothes, her scarves, her perfume, her hairbrushes. She had a small flowered jar, a very pretty one with a curved handle and scalloped lid, that she kept face powder in. And she had a big powder puff that fitted into it.' She glanced up at Jason, and he saw that her eyes had filled with tears. 'Isn't it strange that, although her face is a blur, I can remember, in detail, that jar and puff and the colour of the powder she put on it? Perhaps she was the kind of woman who only put value into her possessions and, even though I was a child, I recognised it. You know, sometimes I wonder why I can't see her anymore. I . . .' and now her voice broke, 'sometimes I wonder where she went.'

All he said was, 'Maggie.'

She had always thought that lovemaking with Jason would arise out of a moment of flirtation or teasing seduction; she had never envisioned that he would take her in his arms out of pity and sympathy and the desire to comfort her. She hadn't known that he would slip into the bed next to her, put his arms around her and kiss the corner of her eye which a tear had dampened. And she had never guessed, not in a million years, that the first emotion she would feel in his arms was an unutterable sadness, a welling up of all the feelings her mother's loss had engendered within her. Maggie hadn't cried when Sandra had left; she'd lifted her small, childish chin and dared anyone to think that she cared, but now she wept her heart out against Jason's shoulder, the crisp shirt beneath her face slowly getting wet, the drumming of his heart providing a steady counterpoint to the erratic rhythm of her crying.

'I'm sorry,' she finally said, lifting her head and reaching for a tissue to wipe her eyes and blow her nose.

'For what?' he asked.

'For dampening your shoulder.'

'It can take it,' Jason said softly, wiping a tear off her face with his thumb. 'I could put a sign on it now—"Maggie Jordan cried here".'

She gave him a small smile. 'You could sell tickets.'

'Hell—I could make an easy million that way.'

Maggie turned her face up to his, her dark lashes damp and spiky, the hint of tears still brimming in her eyes. 'You're nice,' she whispered. 'Has anyone ever told you that?'

His reply was a lowering of his head over hers to bestow upon her mouth a kiss of warm compassion. It began with the touch of his lips, a mere brushing so that she barely tasted their texture. He then kissed her at the V of her throat, along a bared shoulder and then down to the curve of her breast, her nightgown slipping lower and lower until she was exposed to her waistline. He cupped a breast in his hand, caressed the aroused nipple with his fingers and then, pulling her up against him, kissed her mouth fully, his tongue exploring her warmth, her eagerness, her willingness.

When their mouths broke apart, he looked down at her, the gold in his eyes intense and warm. 'There's a certain inequity here,' he said softly.

'What's that?' she whispered.

'You're half-dressed and I'm still wearing my shirt.'

'And you think I should do something about it?'

'Well,' he said, 'we're equals, aren't we?'

Maggie sat up, pushed Jason back on to the bed and, with a maddening slowness, unbuttoned his shirt, taking her time over every button, making sure that her fingers trailed tantalisingly against his skin, and glancing at him now and then to see how he was taking the torture.

'I'll get you for this,' he growled.

'Promise?'

Then, when the shirt was finally unbuttoned, she

pushed aside the edges of it and leaned over him, the waves of her hair swinging forward and brushing over his chest. She licked his skin, running her tongue down the centre line of his torso, tasting the crisp dark hair that covered his muscles, until her mouth reached his belt. Then she gently blew air back the way she had come, making him shiver.

'Promise,' he said huskily, and then next thing Maggie knew, she was flat on her back her nightgown had been dumped unceremoniously on the floor and Jason had her hands pinned above her head so that she lay before him like a captive at a slave auction. Her hair was a reddish-brown fan spread across the pillowcase; her body, tanned except for the brief white triangles made by her bikini, was gold against the sheet. She was naked, exposed and vulnerable beneath his glittering glance.

'Now,' he said silkily, 'an eye for an eye.' He started by putting his mouth to the skin of her upper chest and licked, down through the valley between her breasts, circling her belly-button and making her laugh a bit, across the concavity of her abdomen and then, slowly, very slowly, moving lower. When he reached the soft divide of her, his tongue parted the chestnut curls and Maggie began to tremble, feeling the sensations rise from that point as if it were a sun with beams of heat radiating out in every direction from its burning centre. Jason had, long ago, let go of her wrists, but her arms still lay above her head in posture of submission, and her body was weak, helpless and quivering with anticipation.

Jason lifted his head. 'I could be mean and stop,' he said.

Maggie took a deep breath and said shakily, 'It's not fair.'

'What isn't fair?'

'You still have your pants on.'

'True,' he said with a smile, 'they'll have to go.'

When he slid down beside her again, he was naked, aroused, his body branding her with its heat. Maggie turned slightly and clicked off the light, leaving the room dark except for the cool, white illumination of the moon so that their faces were pale ovals, their bodies dusky shapes.

'I liked the light,' Jason said.

'I'm shy,' she said.

'You?' He was stroking her back, his hand moving up and down her spine, curving around her hip.

'Yes.' Maggie, in turn, was exploring, feeling the parts of him that had been out of bounds before; the muscular strength of his buttocks, the triangle of hair at his hips, the hardness of him.

'Tell me what Nicholas did to you,' he said. 'Tell me why you've been afraid to let me make love to you.'

'He wouldn't touch me,' she whispered.

'Where?'

'You know.'

'Ah—here?' His hand cupped her. 'Why?'

'He said it . . . wasn't normal; that I should be satisfied with . . . just him.'

'And you weren't, were you?'

'No.'

'Oh, Maggie,' Jason said, his voice husky, 'I can't wait to touch you—there. Everywhere.'

And he did. There wasn't a part left to Maggie by the time the night was over that Jason had left untouched, his hands warm, knowing and skilful. She discovered erotic zones she hadn't known she possessed and a height of passion that she hadn't known existed. By means of his mouth and his fingers, Jason brought every nerve ending alive. He toyed with her, he played with her, he made her turn to liquid. He brought her to the brink of orgasm and then pulled her back from it so that each unfulfilled journey was that much more exciting and tantalising. He did it until she begged, pleaded and cried for him to enter her. And when he did, and they moved together in the motions of love, that sun within her seemed to burn hotter, ever hotter, until she reached that moment of explosion when everything ceased but the pure white heat of sensation, and when time stopped, leaving nothing in existence but Jason.

Afterwards, they lay in the dark, the sheet covering their bodies, their arms around one another. They were silent, damp from their exertions and the air was redolent with the musky odour that comes from lovemaking. Jason was on his back with Maggie's head tucked into his shoulder; the entire length of her touching him, one of her knees bent and resting on his legs. He felt the wonderful peace of satiation and that highly contented feeling that comes after glorious sex. It was rare enough, he thought, to have a night like this one and he savoured it, letting the memories of it fill him with a langorous pleasure.

Maggie sighed and pressed herself closer to him. 'Thank you,' she said.

'It was a pleasure, and any time, Madame, just speak up.'

'You sound like a waiter.'

Jason grinned to himself. 'Sex is a bit of a . . . service industry.'

'That's awful,' she said.

He made an aggrieved sound. 'I thought you liked my sense of humour.' And then when he felt her finger running down his chest, he added, 'More?'

Emphatically. 'Uh-uh.'

'Satisfied?'

'Very.'

'Think we can try for a repeat performance some time in the future?'

'I'll take up the issue with the proper authorities,' she said lazily.

There was a comfortable silence then, and Jason idly ran his hand over Maggie's shoulder, enjoying the smoothness of her skin under his hand. He had wondered how she would feel in his arms and the knowledge of it, the reality, pleased him immensely. He had first been attracted to the cool, amused glance of her eyes and her challenging, quick wit. He had then fallen in love with the promise of passion that lay below her aloof surface. Now, he was hooked, crazy for every plane, angle, crevice and curve of her.

'Maggie?'

'Mmmm.'

'I've been thinking about marriage.'

'I know.'

'To you,' he said.

He could feel her face muscles move as she smiled. 'I guessed.'

'But we haven't known one another that long.'

'No.'

'And you don't live in Toronto.'

'No.'

Jason sat up slightly and cleared his throat. 'Maggie, you're not being helpful. This is my first marriage proposal and you're making it difficult.'

Her voice purred. 'Maybe you need practice.'

Jason aimed for formality. 'Darling, will you marry me?'

He could feel a spasm of laughter shake her. 'Make the voice a bit huskier.'

He took a handful of her hair and tugged on it. 'I thought they taught young ladies not to fool around with the male ego.'

'I've never been a lady,' she said, 'and, besides, I flunked that course.'

'Enough of this,' Jason growled and he rolled over on top of her and pinned her to the mattress, his leg coming down between hers, his chest pressing against her breasts. 'Say yes or else.'

'Or else what?'

'Or else . . . I'll make love to you again.'

'God forbid,' she said, laughing. 'All right, anything you say, I surrender.'

Jason buried his face in her neck, luxuriating in the fragrant scent of her hair. 'I can find you a job in Toronto,' he said. 'I've got the feeling that you don't much care about the one you have now. Although you don't have to work if you don't want to.'

'I'd like to work for you,' Maggie said and her voice was shy. 'If you don't mind, that is.'

Jason propped himself up on his elbows and looked down into her face. Surprise mixed in him with a sudden joy. 'Of course, I don't mind,' he said. 'I'd love to have you working for me. You could travel with me and ... Maggie, you've no idea how much I've hated the travelling on my own. I get to stay in some of the world's loveliest cities and I've no one to share them with.'

Maggie wrapped her arms around him. 'Oh, Jason,' she began, but then she hesitated.

'Yes?'

'There's my father. I'm going to have to sort that problem out. He's always been so helpless and dependent on me.'

'He's on his own now,' Jason pointed out.

'I'll have to go home and see how it's really worked. Daniel doesn't communicate things very well. When you meet him, you'll see what I mean.'

Jason rolled over, pulling Maggie around with him so that they were lying side by side, facing one another, their bodies touching at the toes, knees, thighs and chest. He kissed her softly on the lips. 'I want children,' he said.

'I know,' she said. 'So do I.'

'I want a *family*.'

Her arms tightened around him. 'I know that, too.'

'Maggie, are you quite sure about this?'

'Yes.'

'We've only known each other for three weeks.'

'Does that bother you?' she asked.

'No,' he said, and a surge of feeling went through him. It was a glorious, feeling, full of heady triumph and an absolute certainty of the 'rightness' of what he was about to say. For the first time in his life, Jason could say the words and know that he meant them. 'I love you,' he added fiercely, 'I have from the moment I set eyes on you.'

When Maggie woke the next morning, sunlight was pouring in the window, touching on the scatter of clothes on the floor, the tangle of sheets and blankets and the dark gleam of Jason's head beside her. They had not fallen asleep for hours, talking about the future and speculating on their life together. She felt incredibly happy and wanted to sit up, raise her arms to the sky and announce to the world the news of her fabulous fortune. She, Maggie Jordan, was going to marry Jason Hale after an admittedly outrageously short acquaintance; they were going to buy a house outside Toronto that had five bedrooms and, at the very minimum, two fireplaces; they were going to have three children, preferably not all of the same sex. They both liked modern furniture, Persian carpets, super-efficient kitchens, Mozart piano sonatas, light breakfasts and deep movies. As soon as Maggie could make arrangements for her father, resign from her job and pack her belongings, she was going to move into Jason's apartment in Toronto. They'd househunt, work together and, because neither she nor Jason wanted fuss or bother, they planned to have a small, quiet wedding ceremony.

Although she had a great urge to leap out of bed, rouse Jason and make their announcement to Carley and Theo, Maggie knew that she didn't have the heart to wake the man sleeping next to her. He was sleeping so deeply that he had not even stirred despite her motions next to him. His eyes were shut, one hand was tucked under his cheek and his bare shoulder, tanned and bronze, lay above the sheet. Despite the bandage on his head, Maggie thought that he looked like a sleeping god, and she allowed her mind, for a brief second, to slip back to their lovemaking of the night before. She flushed from the memory of it, feeling the warmth of remembered desire invade her once again.

No, she scolded herself, you don't wake up the man you love for more sex when he so obviously needs his sleep. It's not right; he'll think you're insatiable. On the other hand, he might just be thrilled that you want him so badly that. ... No, have a heart, give him a break, wait until noon at least. So Maggie eased herself out of bed, dressed quickly in a pair of shorts and a t-shirt and, slipping out of the room with one last glance and a smile at a completely immobile Jason, shut the door quietly behind her. In the bathroom she brushed her teeth, combed the wild chaos of her hair and, as she put on her watch, discovered that it was almost nine o'clock. God, she had promised to phone Oliver at nine o'clock from the phone booth at Merrick!

Maggie burst out of the bathroom, grabbed her purse from the table in the kitchen where she'd left it last and was rushing past Carley in the living room when the other woman said, 'What's the hurry?'

'I . . . have to pick up some stuff in Merrick,' she said and prayed that Carley wouldn't ask any more questions.

But Carley merely shifted on the couch and, lifting up the pot next to her in an inviting fashion, said, 'I just brewed some coffee.' Theodore was nowhere to be seen, and Maggie could only imagine that he was still sleeping off his bout of the night before.

'I'll have some when I get back.'

'Have a good night?' Carley asked innocently.

Maggie fumbled with her keys. 'Fine.'

'Jason still sleeping?'

'He. . . .' Maggie glanced up, saw the mischief in Carley's face and blushed. 'Like a baby,' she admitted.

'Maggie Jordan-Hale,' Carley reminded her in a teasing voice.

'I'll tell you about it later,' Maggie said as she walked quickly out of the living room. 'I promise.'

Hercules met her at the back door, danced around her legs and whined a bit when he saw her opening the door. He stood expectantly beside the driver's seat after she had got in, his curled tail wagging like crazy, his body blocking the door from closing, a tactic that he used frequently when a car-ride seemed forthcoming. Maggie put her key in the ignition and then saw those pleading brown eyes. Jason said that Hercules loved cars, speed and the rush of wind in his ears. He also, Maggie knew, was convinced that he was being left out of something significant if a car took off without him.

'All right,' she said, climbing out of the car and opening the back door, 'but this is only because we've got to learn to get along together. I don't allow barking, wiggling or rough-housing. Got it?'

Hercules licked her hand as she shut the door.

Love a man and love his dog, Maggie thought as she set out for Merrick, and she hummed a bit, making a little tune out of it. The road rolled out behind the car like a smooth, grey ribbon, and Maggie barely noticed the miles pass by. Her thoughts were all on her return to Dragon's Point, to bringing Jason breakfast in bed; toast, black coffee—he didn't take cream or sugar—and a glass of freshly squeezed orange juice, if they had oranges that is. She'd buy some in Merrick, she decided and then prayed that the convenience store would have some. Maggie imagined herself walking into the bedroom, putting the tray on the bedside table and then slowly—oh so slowly—kissing Jason awake. She'd start by pressing her lips to his forehead, then anointing each eyelid. She'd move her mouth to his bare shoulder next and then, when he opened his eyes and a smile would light the golden depths of his eyes, she would. . . .

The gas station came into sight, breaking into her reverie, and Maggie raced into the gravelled lot, not noticing the large, black sedan that was parked by the building. She brought her car to a stop by the phone booth, opened her purse to get some change and shushed a barking Hercules. 'Silence,' she said. 'Just a short phone call and then we'll be done.' She got out of the car, saw that the Samoyed was not going to be satisfied with staying inside and let him out, adding as she did so, 'No funny business. You're going to have to sit by the booth and wait for me. No running after cars or rabbits and no disappearing. Jason would kill me if I lost you.'

Maggie didn't notice the man getting out of the sedan as she began to head towards the phone booth, and she was quite oblivious to his approach until she heard Hercules growl. Startled, she turned around and then stared at the man walking towards her. He was wearing a grey business suit, a white shirt, a blue tie with small diamonds in it. He had thinning brown hair and a pair of spectacles that were slipping down his nose. When he reached up to push them back, Maggie came to life.

'Oliver!' she exclaimed. 'What are you doing here?'

'I had to talk to you in person, Maggie. Couldn't say what I had to over the phone.'

Maggie began to feel alarmed. 'What is it? What's happened? It's not . . . Daniel, is it?'

'No, not Daniel at all. I'm sorry, I didn't mean to frighten you that way.' Oliver glanced around them; another car had driven in by the gas pumps and an attendant was coming out. 'Let's talk in my car. It's air-conditioned anyway.'

His car was large, had grey upholstery and was driven by a chauffeur, who gave Maggie a small formal nod when she climbed into the back seat. She frowned as she glanced at the back of his neck and threw Oliver a quizzical look. 'What's going on?'

'It was important that I. . . .' He was trying to close the door, but Hercules was standing in the way, whining and looking at Maggie like a bereft orphan. 'Whose dog is this?'

'Jason's,' she said. 'He likes cars.'

'Would he mind if we just had a private . . . yes, I guess he would.' Hercules was barking now, giving Oliver a piece of his mind. 'All right, Danforth, let him in the front, will you?'

Hercules was happily esconced in the seat beside the driver, and Maggie couldn't help smiling a bit. The dog looked so important, sitting beside the very correct Danforth, his posture imitating that of the man, his ears perked forward, his eyes looking through the windshield. His tongue lolled out happily as Danforth turned on the ignition and backed the sedan out of the lot.

Maggie's alarm returned. 'Where are we going?'

'Back to Ottawa.'

'To *Ottawa*?' The car was now moving down the highway in the opposite direction of Dragon's Lake. Confused, Maggie glanced at the road behind them and then turned to Oliver. 'Why?'

His voice was dry and impersonal. 'Something's happening with the drug syndicate. The supplies aren't coming through and they're angry. An empty shipment came in yesterday, and we got a leak through the grapevine that they may be coming up to Dragon's Point today.'

'They may be coming. . . .' She echoed his words again, trying to understand what he was saying. 'Who's they?'

'Listen, Maggie. Hale has stopped bringing in heroin, and the syndicate is mad and out for revenge. I had an idea this might be coming—there was an empty shipment last week and I suspected another one would force them to action. My men moved in to surround the house early this morning. We don't know when they'll hit, but when they come, we'll get them all.'

Maggie glanced at Oliver's well-known face and saw something in it she'd never seen before—a cold satisfaction. A chill seemed to enter her heart. 'But Jason's there and Theodore and Carley!'

'We'll be able to step in before anything happens.'

It may have been over-exposure to spy moves, but Maggie was suddenly able to envision it all. The stakeout, the guns, the tension, the anger, the crash as windows were broken, the screams of the unsuspecting. . . . With horror, Maggie grabbed his arm. 'I've got to go back!'

He shook his head. 'No, I want you safe with me.' He saw her frenzied glance at the car doors and added quietly, 'They're locked. Danforth locks them from the driver's seat.'

Maggie put trembling hands up to her mouth. 'He might get hurt. They all might get hurt.'

'Now, Maggie, this is the only way that I. . . .'

'Jason . . .' she breathed and suddenly discovered that it hurt to take a breath. Her lungs seemed to burn from the effort, and she felt her breath come fast and hard as if she were in an obstacle race; running, running to achieve a goal that could not be met. 'But he. . . .'

'And if it's Hale,' Oliver was saying, 'we'll have the whole thing sewed up tight.'

He was sleeping in her bed, naked and vulnerable, not knowing what was about to descend. She had obeyed Oliver and not told Jason about the phone calls and the suspicions of the police. And by being so obedient and law-abiding, she had put the man she loved into danger. Maggie had visions of him trying to defend himself against an army of faceless thugs or caught between gunfire. Her mind balked at envisioning the ultimate possibilities of disfigurement or death, but her body seemed to have an instinctive understanding of the unthinkable outcomes. Her heart was now pounding her chest, and she had broken out in a cold sweat. She suddenly hated Oliver, hated the way he had so coldly arranged her kidnapping, knowing as he did how she felt about Jason.

'Damn you,' she said between clenched teeth.

But Oliver wasn't listening to her. He was looking out of the window of the car at the passing scenery and, with all the hand-rubbing and complacent satisfaction of a man who has everything under control, was saying, 'The thing is that you're safe. I couldn't let anything happen to you—I'd never be able to forgive myself.'

# CHAPTER NINE

MAGGIE opened the front door of the house and, holding an exuberant Hercules on a leash, stood in the doorway and called to her father.

'Dad! I'm going out. If there are any phone calls . . . Dad!'

Daniel Jordan was working in the den, a room right by the front door, and Maggie could just manage to see him from her vantage point. He was at his desk, writing furiously, and it was obvious that he hadn't heard her words at all. Maggie sighed and stepped out on the front porch, pulling the front door closed behind her. A month away from home had given her a new perspective on Daniel. Although she had lived with him all her life, she had never realised just how deep his absorption with mathematics really was. He hadn't been surprised when she'd returned, delivered unceremoniously on the doorstep by a smiling Oliver, without her car or her baggage but with a strange dog standing at her side. He hadn't noticed her unhappiness or tension. In fact, Maggie was not quite sure if Daniel was actually aware of how long she'd been away. He hadn't missed her at all; Maggie was certain of that.

The housekeeper had come in to clean, do laundry and make dinners, a neighbourhood teenager had mowed the lawn, and the arrangements seemed to have worked out perfectly. Other than a small pile of accumulated bills which Maggie had to pay and a neglected herbal garden in the back, both the house and Daniel were in fine shape. Oh, he'd kissed her when she'd come and asked her how her holiday had gone, but Maggie wasn't sure he'd actually listened to the answers. Her father was like that; you could be talking to him and suddenly notice that, although he appeared to be listening, his mind had gone off into another sphere altogether, that abstract sphere where numbers and equations dominated. Daniel Jordan was a genius at manipulating abstract concepts but, when it came to family, he was something of a disaster.

Maggie wondered why she'd never seen him in quite that light before. Certainly at ten years old, she'd been utterly devoted to him. He had never been the kind of man who had thrown her out of his den or ordered her to be quiet; Daniel's powers of concentration were so strong that he'd never minded if she brought her dolls into his office or chattered at him while he worked. She had always thought there was a sympathy between them, a bond established by the leaving of her mother, but now she saw this perception as a childish wish, a matter of looking at her life with rose-coloured glasses. Daniel had tolerated her company and, while she didn't doubt that he was fond of her in his manner, it could be argued quite reasonably and logically, that he'd used her in a purely selfish way. More and more, Maggie was discovering that she felt a chord of sympathy for her mother. She would never know what the attraction was that had pulled her parents together in the first place, but she suspected that Sandra Jordan had quickly found out that Daniel's mathematics came first, last and foremost.

Maggie allowed Hercules to pull her down the street towards the park that served the neighbourhood. The dog had quickly learned the layout of the neighbourhood and made friends with an assortment of small children and other canine denizens. She knew that he missed Jason; there were times when the Samoyed would just sit and stare at her with those pleading, brown eyes, and she would know just what he was thinking. They were, she thought unhappily, fellow sufferers. A week had gone by since Oliver had taken her away from Dragon's Point, a week that had held fear, uncertainty and misery. She'd gone back to work, only to discover that the reality of her job was worse than her memories of it. She no longer could stand the interminable bureaucratic meetings, the tidal flow of useless memos and the inadequacies of her boss, a man who was given to waffling on decisions and passing the buck whenever he could.

It had helped when Oliver had come to report on the health of Jason and Carley and to comment, with some surprise and not a small bit of chagrin, at the rightness of Maggie's instincts. In fact, he'd apologised to her profusely for not believing her. Jason hadn't been the one that the syndicate was gunning for, after all. It had been Theodore.

'Theodore!' Maggie had said, looking at Oliver in disbelief. 'Theodore was smuggling heroin!'

'For the past year.'

'But. . . .' It wasn't the type of fact that could be assimilated easily. Maggie thought of small, cherubic Theodore with his dimples and neatly combed strands of hair. She thought of his prissiness, his obsessions with small details, his old-fashioned formality. None of it jibed with the fact that Theodore was not only a criminal eagerly sought after by the RCMP, but had also dared the wrath of the mob by deciding not to bring in heroin any more. 'But how?'

'He knew who Jason dealt with in Singapore and the syndicate arranged to have a man at that end pack the boxes of computer boards with heroin. And remember the employee you overheard Jason and Theodore discussing? Sam? He was in charge of unwrapping the computer boards that were imported from Singapore. Theodore got rid of him and replaced him with a drug courier.'

'So he was lying to Jason.'

'Sure. He gave Sam enough money to take a long holiday with his wife—a travelling vacation with no forwarding address. That way the drugs could be

unloaded here and collected without anyone getting
suspicious.'

'And was it Theodore who made that phone call?' she
asked.

'What phone call?'

'In the middle of the night. I heard someone in the
den and I tried to get close to the door, but hit over a
table and lamp.'

Oliver gave her a disgusted look. 'I heard about that
one,' he said. 'Who were you trying to be anyway?
James Bond?'

Maggie was contrite. 'Nancy Drew.'

'It was Theodore.'

'I thought it was Jason because Hercules was quiet.'

'He'd drugged the dog.'

Maggie shook her head in disbelief. 'Why did he do
it?'

'Ah—the motive.' Oliver gave a small nod of his head
as if this were the crux of the whole matter. 'Because of
his wife. He got involved because he wanted to keep her
at home and out of pain. Heroin is one of the best
painkillers known to man, but it's illegal here. He
started by getting it for her, using Hale Enterprises'
money. She, of course, became addicted to it, and he'd
also hired full-time nursing care for her. It was
expensive, and he kept on smuggling the stuff in so that
he could return what he had embezzled.'

'So that's why the idea of Hale Enterprises expanding
made Theodore so nervous?'

'Right, he didn't want Jason looking too closely at
the books. He had, however, finally paid the coffers
back, and he wanted out, only the mob had too good a
thing going with him. They didn't want him to quit.'

It all made sense now, as if a gauzy curtain had been
pulled aside to reveal the action in all its clarity. Maggie
remembered that day she'd sat with Theodore on the
porch at Dragon's Point and he'd been so odd, talking
about Emma with a peculiar urgency and asking her if

she loved someone who was in pain, wouldn't she do everything she could to help that person? Yes, she had answered, not knowing what she was saying, not knowing that she was condoning actions that had begun out of compassion, but had soon got out of hand. By that time, Maggie now understood, Theodore must have realised that he was in over his head. With Emma dead and his debt to Jason paid off, his reason for co-operating with the syndicate no longer existed. The mob, however, had not been about to let him off the hook so easily.

'Poor Theo,' she said. 'How is he?'

'He had a heart attack when the action began,' Oliver said.

'A heart attack!'

'He's all right,' Oliver assured her. 'He's out of intensive care at the Toronto General. Apparently, he collapsed the minute he saw a face at the window. There was a bit of a scuffle but it didn't last long after my men got in.'

'I think he knew it was coming,' Maggie said slowly. 'He'd been acting so strangely the day before.'

Oliver nodded. 'I suspect he'd told his contact that he wasn't going to co-operate any more and he'd been threatened.'

'What's going to happen to him?'

'Well, he's a sick man, he's co-operated with us fully and, God knows, the circumstances were extenuating. I suspect the judge will be fairly lenient.'

'And Carley . . .?'

'She had locked herself in her bedroom. She'd had a bit of a shock, but it seems to have done her some good. She's checked herself into a drug rehabilitation centre, and she was quite willing to give us information. We've got David Moss in custody; it seemed he had a connection at a drug firm who was supplying him with stuff. We got the connection, too.' Oliver rubbed his hands together. 'Not a bad operation.'

'And . . . Jason?'

'A good man; he was quick. He got to Theodore in a hurry and was giving him mouth-to-mouth when my men arrived. Probably saved his life. He and I have been going over the deal that Theodore had worked out with the people in Singapore. He flew over to meet with the police there. If we're lucky, we'll cut off the heroin traffic at that end.'

'So Jason's in Singapore.'

'He'll be there for a bit.' Oliver noticed the look on her face. 'Now, don't worry, Maggie, he'll be back soon.'

'I just wondered. . . .'

'And I told him all about you,' Oliver said, clearly satisfied with the way he was tying all the ends together in neat, little bows. 'Besides, you've got his dog; he's bound to show up soon.'

'Yes,' Maggie had said, but Oliver's words hadn't comforted her. She had expected to hear from Jason right away; she had thought he'd call her the minute he'd been near a telephone. She couldn't understand the week of silence from a man who had told her he loved her, asked her to marry him and had been an ardent and tender lover. And Maggie didn't think his trip to Singapore was much of an excuse. There were telephones in Singapore and long-distance lines. She *had* tried to phone him; she'd called his home in Toronto, his business office and finally Carley's apartment. The constant, unanswered ringing of telephones and a secretary who had repeatedly told her that 'Mr Hale wasn't available' had finally driven her to quit, but her isolation was agonising, and Maggie had come to the uncomfortable conclusion that something in her relationship with Jason had gone dreadfully wrong. The problem was—she didn't know what it was.

Still, as Oliver had said, there was Hercules. The dog was now bounding through the park, running back and forth on the grass, sniffing here, there and everywhere.

He ran with his tongue hanging out and in no perceptibly organised fashion. It was clear to anyone who watched him that, to Hercules, life was intoxicating and exhilarating, Jason or not. Except for the occasional sad look, he had adapted to Maggie's life as if he belonged there. He had already discovered a favourite sleeping spot—a spot in the dining room where the sun came in and warmed the floor—and his eating habits were certainly not those of a dog in a decline. Maggie had become quite fond of Hercules; his presence made her feel close to Jason, and she'd come to think of him as a form of 'insurance policy'. Her possession of him would bring Jason to Ottawa.

When Hercules had finally expended so much energy that he returned to Maggie, his sides visibly heaving from his exertions, she hooked the leash to his collar and they made their way back to the house. Daniel looked up as Maggie came in the doorway and said, 'There was a phone call for you.'

'Who was it?' she asked, removing the leash from Hercules' neck.

Daniel was still at his desk in the den in a pose that Maggie had been familiar with since childhood. He was a thin man, already stooped, with long narrow hands, and he was bent over one pile of papers while three others were stacked up on either side of him. Pencils littered the top of the desk, and the chair nearby held a leaning tower of books and journals. The only time that Daniel was not at his desk was when he was teaching or sleeping. He generally took his meals there as well, eating whatever Maggie put in front of him.

He had already turned back to the book he was reading. 'A man,' he said absentmindedly.

Maggie straightened up and felt her heart start to thud. 'Did he leave his name?'

Daniel took his eyeglasses off, rubbed his forehead, ran his narrow, bony hand through the wild fringe of white hair on his head and put his glasses back on. 'He did say something,' he replied in a distracted tone. 'I should have jotted it down, it's escaped me now.'

Maggie tried to stifle her impatience. 'It might be important,' she said.

'Let me think ... now, what did he say his name was?' Daniel had been looking at Maggie, but now he glanced back down at the book before him.

There were a few minutes of silence while Maggie stood in the doorway of the den, nervously twisting the leash in her hand while she waited for Daniel to collect his thoughts. Finally, she realised that he'd forgotten all about her and was once again absorbed in his reading.

She sighed with impatience. 'Dad! Who was it?'

Daniel reluctantly turned his head. 'Can't remember. He didn't say much, just told me to tell you he had phoned. Maybe it was that . . .' He searched in the air for the name he sought. '. . . Nicholas.'

'Nicholas!'

But Daniel was already buried in his book, and Maggie knew that her chances of getting any more information out of him were hopeless. She followed Hercules into the kitchen, fed him and then wandered out into the backyard where she tried to make some sense out of the herbs she had planted there early in the summer. Although it was September already, the day promised to be a hot one, and she could feel the heat of the mid-day sun beating down on her bare shoulder blades. She was barefoot, wearing a white halter top and a pair of jeans, and she had tied her hair back into an untidy ponytail. As she tugged at an overgrown bush of basil, she muttered, 'Nicholas,' under her breath and in a tone of disgust. Not that she actually thought it had been Nicholas who had called; she rather suspected that Daniel, under pressure, had pulled that name out of a hat. It was just that the idea of Nicholas was abhorrent to her. Whatever longings she might have nurtured about him had been effectively eliminated by her feelings for Jason. Once, she had secretly hoped that

Nicholas would want to see her again; now, the thought of him completely turned her off.

The chives were thick but flattened, and Maggie suspected that the neighbour's cat, a large calico, had been taking afternoon naps in it. She grumbled over that and then turned her attention to the leeks which, thank heavens, were thriving. When she considered the effort she'd put into planting them, a backbreaking chore that had. . . .

'Maggie.'

The voice hit chords of memory, shadings and tones that she knew so well. Maggie whirled around to find Jason standing on the patio. He looked every bit as wonderful as she remembered him, dressed in beige slacks, a pale blue shirt, his black hair gleaming in the sun, his face beautiful in the light and shadow cast by the old maple that stood at the back of the house. She couldn't see the look in his eyes or even read the expression on his face from this distance. She saw only the stillness of him, as if he were waiting for something, a sign from her perhaps, a signal of love. She forgot all about her worries and apprehensions, and a happiness rushed into her, transforming the day from its ordinary dimensions into something far more different. The air seemed to shimmer with excitement; the sun's heat measuring, beat for beat, the rising warmth within her. The suburban sounds, of a truck driving past, a child calling to another, seemed to disappear until nothing remained but the humming rhythm of the blood pulsing in her veins and the silence between them that carried, for her, the words they'd exchanged, the murmurings of lovers, those sweet phrases whispered in the dark.

'Jason,' she finally said, her voice breathless. And then she rushed towards him, arms outstretched, not caring about the dishevelled state of her hair, her dirty fingers, patched jeans and bare feet. She ran towards him as if she had wings, lightly and with a heady anticipation of being in his arms once again. She ran towards him with all the conviction of a woman in love that the man standing so still on the patio stones was hers and hers alone.

But when Maggie reached Jason, she stopped, caught up short by the sudden knowledge that his stillness came, not from any reined-in eagerness to embrace her, but from a deep-seated anger. His jaw was clenched tightly; the golden eyes glittered at her like miniature fires. There was also a look of fatigue about him and a new thinness that put faint hollows in his cheeks and made the aquiline ridge of his nose sharper, but her awareness of this was overwhelmed by the fury burning in him. Maggie had never seen Jason like this before, and she was frightened—badly.

But his voice gave none of his emotions away; it was cool, formal, polite. 'I've come for Hercules.'

'He's . . . in the house.'

'Thanks for taking care of him for me.'

'I . . . he was no problem.'

The day swept back in on her in all its mundane aspects. A back door slammed on a nearby house, the sound of a car radio blared noisily as the vehicle turned the corner. All the enchantment that Maggie had first felt on seeing Jason had died away to be replaced by the prosaic realities of life. She was hot and sweaty from working in the sun; the man before her was a stranger she had met only four weeks before; her fears had come back and were magnified fourfold . . . The fact that she had known Jason well and intently did not seem to alter the atmosphere between them. It was cold, aloof and tense with an undercurrent of dislike.

Jason stood aside so that Maggie could pass and lead him into the house, and she slowly walked up the steps, feeling him behind her and knowing that her legs were trembling. She desperately wished that she could stop them from shaking, but she didn't know how, and she was afraid that it would spread and become visible. She gripped her hands into fists and set her face in a mask that was uncaring, emotionless, bland.

'Here he is,' she said, pointing to Hercules who had finished his lunch and who could now be seen spread out on his favourite spot in the dining room, fast asleep.

'Hey, Herc,' Jason said and gave a little whistle. The effect was galvanising. The dog had no sooner opened his eyes and seen Jason before he was on his feet, barking wildly and jumping up on Jason, trying to lick his face. 'Down,' Jason said, vigorously rubbing Hercules' ears. 'Down, boy.'

Maggie hadn't thought she had any more tears to shed, but she felt a new supply rise at the sight of Jason and his dog. It was devastating to discover that the man she loved had no feeling for her, but a wealth of affection for his dog. She turned away so that Jason wouldn't see her face and said in the lightest tone she could muster, 'If I'd known it only took a whistle. . . .'

So, it had all been a fake, Jason thought as he soothed Hercules down, his fingers gripping the thick white fur at the dog's neck. He had wondered about the look on her face when she'd stood up from her gardening and that rush up to him as if she were delighted to see him again. A fake, just as all the rest of it had been; the flirtation, the lovemaking, the talk of marriage and children. She had lied to him, led him on and then betrayed him. The anger that raged within him was conveyed to Hercules who whimpered slightly and then licked his face.

When Jason had woken that morning and found Maggie gone, he hadn't been alarmed. He had been so tired and slept so heavily that it was already late, and he knew she was an early riser. He had smiled to himself when he saw the nightgown strewn on the floor and his own clothes draped on odd pieces of furniture, and he had happily sung his way through an invigorating shower. His head no longer ached the way it had, and he felt an extraordinary energy as if lovemaking with

Maggie had enriched the very blood that ran through his veins.

He'd been surprised to discover that she wasn't in the kitchen and that, in fact, her car was gone. Carley had had no idea why she'd driven to Merrick, but Jason had shrugged that off and assumed she'd be back soon. That nonchalance had worn off within an hour, and by that time, he'd been pacing the floor of the living room, driving Carley crazy and making Theodore, who was suffering from a bad hangover, groan in pain. Finally, just when he had decided to take Carley's car and head into Merrick, convinced that Maggie had been involved in an accident and was hurt or, even worse, dead, it had happened.

Two faces had appeared at the window, a door had been thrown open, a loud voice had said 'We're looking for Wolf,' and suddenly a rifle had been pointed in his direction. Jason had hardly assimilated this when four other men had rushed into the house and a fight began. Only one gunshot went off, but the sound of it was ear-splitting and a spiderweb of cracks appeared in one of the large panes of glass that overlooked the lake. A lamp was knocked over, its bulb shattering, and a chair fell on its side with a crash. Carley had screamed and run into her bedroom; Theodore had clasped his chest and collapsed in the living room. Jason, who had instinctively ducked behind a chair when he'd seen the rifle, immediately ran to Theodore and, recognising the symptoms of a heart attack, had started to give him rescusitation.

Although Jason had felt as if it were going on for ever, the entire event was over and done with in seconds. The thugs were subdued and taken to a squad car, and a policeman had come to help Jason with Theodore. When Jason finally stood up to assess the damage, Dragon's Point looked like a scene out of a thriller or television police series. The house was surrounded by police cars, with their lights flashing and sirens going. A constable came up to him, asked him if he were Jason Hale and then announced he was under arrest. It took Jason half-an-hour to sort out why he was under arrest and, with the added testimony of one of the thugs, to convince the constable that he wasn't the man they were looking for. He was still reeling from the realisation that Theodore had been using Hale Enterprises to smuggle heroin, when the thought of Maggie hit him.

'There's another woman living here,' he said, frantically grabbing the constable's arm. 'She's disappeared.'

The constable had taken out a notebook and was writing notes down in it. 'Maggie Jordan?' he asked.

Jason stared at him and felt his mouth go dry. So there had been an accident. 'Is she all right? Was she hurt? How did . . .?'

'She's fine.'

'Where is she?'

'On her way to Ottawa with the boss.'

Jason wondered why he couldn't understand; he felt stupid and lumpish. 'The boss?'

'Head of the Narcotics Squad.'

Jason formed his words very carefully. 'Why didn't he bring her back here?'

The constable had shrugged and answered, 'He wanted her out of danger. She was working for us. A drug informer.'

And Jason had felt himself echoing and repeating those words, helplessly and disbelievingly, 'A drug informer . . . a drug informer . . .' while all the ramifications of Maggie's actions and words began to come home to him. The pain of betrayal had been incredible; he had thought he might double over from it, but instead he had held himself rigid, had packed his suitcase, had driven back to Toronto with a nervous and remorseful Carley and had immediately put his business back in order. Not even his meeting with

Oliver, who had explained Maggie's role during that month, made Jason's anger ease. He didn't care that she hadn't known the attack was coming or that Oliver had manipulated it so that she wouldn't be there. It was the realisation that she had used him that made Jason's blood boil. And he was now convinced that most of her actions had been designed to either elicit information from him or keep him so bemused with her that he wouldn't guess what she was really after.

As Jason glanced at her, he didn't see the woman he had held and loved in his arms, he saw a stranger, tall and beautiful, who had lied, kept secrets and abused his trust. He had enjoyed watching her rush up to him and then stop in bewilderment, reading the fury in his eyes. Jason wanted to hurt Maggie; he wanted her to feel the pain he had felt and to know the clawing anguish of betrayal.

'Come on, Herc,' he said. 'Let's go home.'

Maggie heard those words and the finality in Jason's voice, and the bottom of her world seemed to drop out from beneath her with a sickening rush. She had turned away from him, and now she grabbed on to a kitchen counter, feeling a dizziness come over her and knowing that, if she didn't hold on to something, she would collapse. She could feel her blood draining away from her face and knew that Jason would see her pallor if she looked directly at him. To avoid that, Maggie reached for the leash which was hanging on a hook by the back door and said, 'Here's his leash. I had to buy one for him.'

'I'll pay you back.'

'Oh, no, that's not necessary.'

It couldn't be helped; their eyes met then and Maggie was shocked by what she saw in Jason's face. Beyond the anger was a mass of hurt and pain and unhappiness, and she instinctively reacted to it, forgetting everything that had passed between them in the past few minutes and wanting only to soothe away the deep lines that ran between his mouth and nose, the sad curve of his mouth. The leash dropped from her hand, and she reached up and gently touched his cheek.

He stepped back as if her fingers had burned him. 'Don't touch me,' he said with snarl.

Her voice was soft. 'Why?'

'Why!' It was the question Jason had expected, and it threw him off his stride.

Maggie swallowed nervously. 'I . . . we were. . . .'

'Lovers?' he asked harshly. 'Was that what we were?'

'I . . . thought so.'

'Anything to find out my secrets. Wasn't that it, Maggie? Didn't you want to know every little detail so you could telephone the police? Did you tell them how I made love? Was that part of your job?'

Shock enveloped her. Maggie stared at him in disbelief. 'Didn't Oliver explain . . .?'

'Oh, he explained all right,' Jason said harshly. 'He told me all about it.'

'But I knew it wasn't you! I *told* him it couldn't be you.'

'And what was the night we had together—extra research?'

'Jason!' His name came out of her mouth like a wail as he turned away from her. She watched the rigid line of his back as he leaned over, picked up the leash and attached it to Hercules' collar. He straightened up and began to stride out of the kitchen, and it was then that Maggie realised that he fully intended to walk out of the house and her life without even looking back.

'Jason,' she said, her voice broken and pleading, 'I love you.'

He stopped, but his back was to her and she couldn't see his face. 'What?' he asked in a low voice.

'I love you. I . . . thought you knew that.'

Jason turned slowly. 'Say it again.'

Maggie's hands were out in front of her in a gesture of entreaty. 'I fell in love with you, and that's when I knew in my heart that you weren't what Oliver said you were. I begged him to change his mind, but he was so convinced that you were guilty that nothing I would say worked. But *I* knew you were innocent.'

'Why didn't you tell me what was going on?'

'Oliver made me promise not to tell, and it didn't seem important to me anymore. I know that sounds ridiculous, but I was caught up in life at Dragon's Point and Oliver's crazy suspicions didn't really seem to touch us. I didn't know it was Theodore either. I was too busy with . . . you, Jason, to care what Oliver was doing. And I knew it would be all right . . . that somehow, he would find out what I already knew – that you couldn't be involved in drugs.'

His voice was light, conversational, as if the facts were only slowly being absorbed. 'You never told me, you know.'

'Told you what?'

'That you loved me.'

Maggie's eyes were wide, blue, astonished. 'I didn't?'

'No,' he said. 'You didn't.'

She was crying then and half-laughing as she threw herself at him, wrapping her arms around his neck. Hercules started to bark as Jason pulled Maggie up into a tight embrace and buried his face in her hair.

'I love you,' she said. 'Do you believe me? Do you?'

His voice was muffled; she could feel his lips moving against her neck. 'You'll never know,' he said, 'what you put me through, what I thought. All those things we said to one another . . . those words. Oh, Maggie, I thought you had lied to me, made it all up. I suffered agonies this past week, and I hated you for it. When I came here today, I wanted to kill you.' He lifted his head and put his hands to her throat, the warm fingers encircling the slender column of her neck. 'I wanted to strangle you,' he said, the golden-green eyes smiling down at her. 'Slowly.'

Her voice was teasing, playful. 'I'll let you do other things to me slowly.'

'Will you?' His mouth brushed hers, his tongue licked at her lips.

'Mmmm.'

He kissed her then fully, his mouth exploring hers with all the warmth and passion she had remembered and longed for. Maggie closed her eyes and revelled in the feel of him against her, the crispness of his hair in her fingers, the smell of him, the sensation that she'd come home again. They might have gone on like that for hours if Hercules hadn't intervened, his cold nose trying to nuzzle between their knees, a small whimper in his throat.

'What are we going to do with this dog?' Jason asked, looking down at Hercules with a mixture of irritation and affection.

Maggie ruffled the fur on top of Hurcules' head. 'Not give him a key to our bedroom for starters,'

'Maggie, I have an apology to make.'

'You do?'

'For all that heavy-handed psychological analysis – about your mother. Of course, I didn't know you were fighting me off because you thought I was dealing in drugs.'

'But you were right,' she said. 'I've carried a lot of emotional baggage around because she left me. I've been cold, afraid of loving other people, fearful of committing myself to anyone. I kept myself isolated from relationships; I was always afraid of marriage because I didn't think I'd know how to be a wife and mother.'

Jason gently pushed back a tendril of her hair that had fallen across her cheek. 'And now?'

Her eyes were a soft blue, wide and longing. 'I don't think I'll ever rid myself of worrying about it,' she said slowly, 'but I want very much to be the right wife for you and a good mother to the children we have.'

He cupped her face between his hands. 'I'm not worried about you being a good mother,' he said, 'and as for my wife – hell, you passed the test with flying colors.'

'What test?'

Jason grinned at her. 'It's vulgarly known as a 'roll in the hay.'

'Oh,' she said, bristling slightly, 'that wasn't my test. That was yours.'

'Really? And did I pass?'

Her voice was severe, schoolmarmish. 'You're in the ninety-eighth percentile.'

'Oh? And just what happened to the other two percent?'

Maggie gave him a long look. 'It requires re-testing.'

'I see.' Jason pulled her up to see him once again. 'In that case, why don't we . . . .'

A short, dry cough separated them, and they both turned to see Daniel Jordan standing in the doorway of the kitchen, his eyes blinking and slightly bewildered behind the round frames of his spectacles.

'Dad,' Maggie said, 'have you met . . .?'

Both Jason and Daniel spoke at the same time.

'I introduced myself when . . .'

'I met the young man when he came in.'

Maggie gave Jason a smile and, linking her arm though his, turned to her father. 'We're getting married,' she said and then waited, not knowing what Daniel would do or say. Would he complain that he was losing a perfect housekeeper or be horrified that she was marrying a stranger? Or would he simply accept the *fait accompli* and congratulate them, wishing them good luck and best wishes?

She should have known better, of course. She should have known that it was too much to hope that Daniel, mathematician and deep thinker, would act out of character. He cleared his throat and waved a distracted hand in the air as if brushing at flies. 'Maggie, you know that book, the one on differential equations? I haven't been able to find it anywhere and I wondered if you moved it when you dusted the other day.'

Jason looked down at Maggie in surprise and she gave him an I-told-you-so glance. 'Dad, I said—we're getting married.'

Daniel blinked at her again as if she'd dragged him, reluctantly, out of the depths of an all-encompassing train of thought. 'Married? Well, I suppose it's a good idea. You're certainly old enough. And Nicholas seems like a fine, young man. Now, have you seen that book?'

Maggie couldn't help it; she laughed and discovered that Jason was laughing with her. Daniel stared at them for a second and then wandered out of the kitchen.

When she finally caught her breath, Maggie said, 'Welcome to the family—Nicholas.'

Jason shook his head. 'Will he ever figure it out?' he asked, pulling Maggie back in his arms.

She reached up, kissed the enticing curve of his mouth and said, 'In about ten years,' she said, 'if we're lucky.'

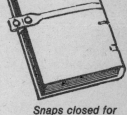